T0022047

After Tonight, Everything Will Be Different

Adam Gnade

Praise for Adam Gnade's *After Tonight, Everything Will Be Different*

"*After Tonight, Everything Will Be Different* is an excellent novel, an energetic tale of ambition, sorrow, and American hunger. Anthony Bourdain meets Roberto Bolaño. I'd like to say I read it all in one sitting, but the truth is that I had to stand up halfway through and walk down the street to get a burrito. When somebody writes as artfully about food as Gnade does, you just can't help yourself." **-Nathaniel Kennon Perkins, author of *Wallop***

"*After Tonight, Everything Will Be Different* is a love letter to the ephemeral, to San Diego, to a place and time Gnade once knew and loved deeply. Reading this book is like sharing a delicious meal with a friend, and having a deep, hours long conversation that food can bring about. Gnade makes it easy to listen to him. I read this book while scrambling eggs, devouring pasta, waiting in a drive through line, and washing the dishes. I didn't want to put it down. These were not my friends Gnade was describing. It was not my family nor my childhood, and yet, I felt a bond. I wanted to know what happened to these fleeting faces. I wanted to share a burrito with them and listen. This book is a way of splitting a steaming, grease-stained bag of burritos with a friend while staring out at this 'shit world.' Gnade names it as such and gives readers sights of death, pain, and self-ishness as proof. But through and through, he hangs onto his optimism. The world contains a glimmer of hope in it, he urges. If you look for it. And Gnade looks deeply. He takes readers down the back paths of his memory and allows them to pull back a curtain to peek inside. Childhood is spread across the scene, and then adulthood. Childhood moments are catalogued with Gnade's reflections on life. He speaks to the reader, the eternal *you*, with a sense of earnestness that tinges on desperation at times. He is trying to get through to the reader, to *you*, and to really be heard. Gnade is urging a more steadied sense of attention; a care and curiosity for the world, and a sense that there is magic out there—even if it is hiding. This book will make you sentimental for days past. You will want to call your old friends up and tell them you love them, or at least invite them over for a meal. It will make you wish you were from San Diego. I am. And the burritos are just as good as Adam describes them." **-Lora Mathis, artist and author of** *The Women Widowed to Themselves*

"*After Tonight, Everything Will Be Different* is like a culinary *On the Road*, a salsa-stained Moleskine, a manifesto from the heart and stomach who are both yearning for the same warmth. In Gnade's deeply affecting memoir, food is the common ground for outsiders, punks, and misfits whose only loyalties lie with each other and their choice of red or green sauce. This is a journey where every cheap burrito, slice of pizza, and square of American cheese tells a story of heartbreak, sadness, love, and hope." **-Ryan Bradford, author of** *AwkwardSD*

"*Stay Hungry*, says Springsteen, and that's what Adam Gnade says with this book. *After Tonight, Everything Will Be Different* is all about hunger, and it will make you hungry, too. Hungry for hope and change and joy, hungry for friendship and love and moments of human connection, hungry for the memories of breaking bread with loved ones and strangers alike, hungry for *experience*. And also for food. Lots and lots of food. I could definitely use some fish tacos or a chile relleno burrito right about now. **-Jessie Lynn McMains, author of** *Wisconsin Death Trip* **and** *The Loneliest Show On Earth*

"Those of us raised around Italian immigrants know the only way to truly gain a grandma's trust was to be a good eater. Your brother might make good grades or you get busted being drunk at school, but things were good with the elder crew if they liked your appetite when the pot came off the stove. *After Tonight* is guided by the appetite of a good eater. It's not exclusive like the worst kind of foodie tales you overhear in city restaurants. All the self-hate and pointed doom—how it's in here—I love because most food writing doesn't allow it a seat. Adam understands the luxury of a Kraft Single on a fridge's empty shelf, or that a supermarket bakery sheet cake could be your only friend, could be your Grandmother when you need it to be. Eating's a complicated gift and a feast could be remembering your ghosts." **-Rich Baiocco, cook and zine writer, author of *Death in a Rifle Garden***

"*After Tonight, Everything Will Be Different* is a heartfelt continuation of Adam Gnade's personal mythology. It is also your own. In it he compiles dispatches on the back of iridescent taco shop receipts that your friends will read at your funeral. Oh what a joy to have lived, to have eaten, and to remember it at all." **-Nick Bernal, Burn All Books**

"With *After Tonight, Everything Will Be Different*, Adam captures what food means as an emotional anchor, and as a communal ritual. He explores memory and shared experiences between transient characters through the meals they consume together. Sometimes food is the only constant in a terrifying world that's always changing faster than we can process." **-Jon Nix, director of *Beyond Barricades* and *Don't Fall in Love with Yourself***

"Adam Gnade picks up Woody Guthrie's hoping machine and makes it sing his own song. He makes bad feelings feel good—wide-eyed with wonder, but crystal-clear. I want to eat every meal in this book while I laugh and cry." **-Dmitry Samarov, author of *Old Style***

"Adam Gnade deftly captures the starkness of wading through life on the crux of happiness or despair, never fully falling in to either, and he does so with the same dreamy, exquisite detail by which he serves up meal after meal. It's a love song for San Diego food (reading while hungry is a specific torture). It's also a love song for an entire city and a love song for the people who call it home—and those who once did, and those who refuse to. Gnade's restless, melancholy storytelling had me grieving characters even when they were right there in front of me. And sometimes there's joy: a sincere, engulfing hope. *After Tonight, Everything Will Be Different* is memory, it's honesty, it's survival, it's hunger, it's home." **-Julia Dixon Evans, author of *How to Set Yourself on Fire***

"Food is a lifeline often invisible and undervalued and as is always the case, human connection is the main course. As someone that has long since ignored these lifelines, here is a bold, yet delicate reminder that we are surrounded by these leads, these treasures. If only we'd reach out and meet them halfway. Gnade has been channeling human empathy in his writing for years and in *After Tonight, Everything Will Be Different*, he has finally perfected his emotive spell." **-Michael J. Seidlinger, author of *Runaways: A Writer's Dilemma***

"Make sure you eat before you read this; you'll starve if you don't. Not since his first novel *Hymn California* has Adam Gnade captured so well the energy and joy and pain of youth. Yes, this is a love song to food—how most of the time it's the best thing in our lives—but this is also about survival. Absurd, hilarious, and hard. If you ever wanted to know how Gnade earned the wisdom to battle the Big Sad, you'll find a trail of breadcrumbs in these stories. One answer: Don't eat American cheese slice tacos." **-Bart Schaneman, author of *The Green and the Gold***

"People don't talk about food like this. It's stripped of pretension, and appreciates what we consume and what consumes us. In this book, there's freedom in a food truck burrito, despite the oppression in everything else. Food is love. And Adam Gnade wants you to know you are loved." **-Joshua Bohnsack, author of *Shivers***

"Adam Gnade is as good as anyone at capturing the fleeting beauty of great food—the delicacy of an unforgettable eggplant parmesan, the bright chemistry of butter brushed across seared sourdough—but thankfully, his proud, broken characters find as much joy in lowlife bars as in highbrow restaurants. They know the profound pleasures of dipping hot, salt-slathered French fries into a Wendy's Frosty, and they practice scientifically proven procedures for deconstructing Oreos in order to enjoy maximum Oreo-ness. When combined with Gnade's tattoo-worthy maxims ("The more taco shops your neighborhood has, the finer your life will be"), the result is a novel about how eating and drinking—with honest enthusiasm, with easy laughter, with those we love—binds us together. There are few places better to be than with the dreamers and cynics of *After Tonight, Everything Will Be Different*, whether they're quietly relishing a hard-won, fresh-caught meal on a cold beach against a storm-darkened sea, or swigging warm tequila from an old canteen, sprawled across the backseat in a car full of friends, heading to places unknown." **-Erik Henriksen, *Portland Mercury*, *The Stranger***

"Adam Gnade is a wildly unique kind of author who is both raw and thoughtful. He brings a sense of object permanence in our currently erratic world. *After Tonight, Everything Will Be Different* is simply great. It needs to be devoured in a way that can only be described within the pages of this book." **-Mallory Smart, author of *The Only Living Girl In Chicago***

"Ever had your heart broken by some small casual cruelty? Do you remember the taste of something you know the name and smell of, but not the feel of it in your mouth? Has a burrito ever stood between you and the abyss and been enough to keep you from that freefall? Do you long for hearth and home and friends at the table? If so, this book is the nourishment you need." **-Nicole Morning, author of** *Selftitled*

"Sometimes, a lovingly made tomato sandwich fills the existential hole inside of us (if only for a while). The fanciest meal hearkens back to your first real heartbreak, while memories of a 99-cent breakfast on a corner in NYC forever radiates the purest warmth. This isn't a conventional book about food: it's a beautiful eulogy to all the dishes that have gotten Adam Gnade through the thick of it, for better or worse. *After Tonight, Everything Will Be Different* is both romantic and raucous, tender and sharp-witted, in the way that only the best love letters are." **-Becky DiGiglio, photographer,** *Born Upside Down*

"Dragging your hands across coarse bark, you're reminded of the importance of a life that breathes for the world. Reading Gnade, you feel a palm close around yours and are reminded of tenderness. Not since Steinbeck has a writer captured what it is to be with and for the world pressing against your skull." **-Giaocomo Pope, Neutral Spaces founder, author of** *Chainsaw Poems & Other Poems*

"No matter the hour, I am my most alert—most alive—when reading Adam Gnade's impactful novel. I was not around in many of the eras depicted, nor lived in any of its locations, but I so heavily related to the characters' despair and self-loathing that I flinched. Gnade's prose does not romanticize description nor pain, but there's succinct and eloquent beauty amid the lobster carcasses and old Halloween candy. Food as sustenance in a

myriad of ways—from bonding, validation, to the sole thing keeping you going. Yet in these dark, harsh realities, there are shafts of hope breaking through, that may help you live in the increasingly chaotic world we are all in now. Like it does for me. Different angles that allow you to see there is an actual surface to afloat despite your current drowning. Reading this made me want to reconnect with old friends, to try to cook these favorite meals, to better savor the food made by my loved ones, to fly out to San Diego and eat a chorizo burrito while watching the tide pools at Sunset Cliffs. The only thing I found wrong was this wasn't longer, but there's a bevy of interconnected novels and records to explore, once I'm done rereading about that fish taco. It's 4 o'clock in the morning, but Gnade makes me want to write, and that's the highest compliment you can pay any author."
-Eileen Ramos, poet, Hello America Stereo Cassette contributor

OTHER BOOKS BY ADAM GNADE

FICTION
Hymn California
Caveworld
Locust House
This is the End of Something But It's Not the End of You
Float Me Away, Floodwaters
The Internet Newspaper

NON-FICTION
The Do-It-Yourself Guide to Fighting the Big Motherfuckin' Sad
Simple Steps to a Life Less Shitty

Three One G/Bread & Roses Press

Bread & Roses Press
P.O. Box 410
Chelsea, MI 48118

Three One G
P.O. Box 178262
San Diego, CA 92177
www.ThreeOneG.com

ISBN: 978-1-939899-98-9

First printing, January 5th, 2022
Second printing, April 2nd, 2022
Third printing, December, 17th, 2022
Fourth printing, January 5th, 2023
Fifth printing, October 5th, 2023

Edited by Jessie Duke
Research assistance from Elizabeth Thompson
Cover photo by Becky DiGiglio
Cover model Justin Pearson
Art design and layout by Bran Black Moon
Chapter photos by Becky DiGiglio, Adam Gnade, &
Reira Moon.
Chapter composites by Bran Black Moon

Printed in the United States of America
5 7 9 11 13 12 10 8 6
After Tonight, Everything Will Be Different
Adam Gnade

After Tonight, Everything Will Be Different
Adam Gnade

"First we eat, then we do everything else"
-M.F.K. Fisher

"Lisa says, hey baby
for just one little smile
I'll sing and play for you
for the longest while"
-the Velvet Underground

EGGPLANT PARMESAN,
OR THE PART IN THE BOOK
THAT BEGINS AT THE END OF THE STORY

****

There is a difference in the way you run when you are being chased. It's not the same as jogging and it's not the same as all the running we did in high school just a few years ago, bored but dutiful, circling the red earth track in our charcoal gray t-shirts and flimsy black shorts. There is a difference in the way you run at night in an unfamiliar place and there is a difference in the way you run when the crime you are committing is an act of joy—a crime you've told yourself is a righteous one.

It's the end of the century and Chente Ramirez and I are running down a moonlit side-street in Little Italy, holding our plates of eggplant parmesan out in front of us. We've just dine 'n' dashed, and it's a lovely, warm San Diego night, and I am eating with my hands as I run because the food we stole from Marco Antonio's fake fucking Italian Piazza is just as good as Chente said it would be.

As we run, I can smell the marinara and the fresh basil, and beyond that the harbor, the smell of the bay—saltwater and boat diesel and hot tar. (Then, for the smallest second as we pass a row of darkened houses, it's the candy scent of night-blooming jasmine. There is a whole world coming at you as you run in the night. There is a world everywhere around you, and you are moving within it like an arrow shot through a forest of dark trees.)

Chente runs ahead of me now, effortless, godlike, hands held out in front of him—his plate of food steady and level like it's sitting on a table.

At that moment I notice he's taken a piece of bread.

Balanced on the very edge of his plate is a golden-brown roll of Marco Antonio's garlic bread, and it stays perfectly still as Chente runs.

It's like one of those late-night commercials you see

when you've been up for a million hours and you can't sleep, only you're too tired to do anything productive, and the woman on screen in her silver negligee jumps happily on a bare mattress like she's skipping rope. At her feet is a full wine glass that stands as still as a statue or a stone tower.

It's like Chente is the happy, jumping woman and the roll is the unshakable glass of wine and I guess the ground is the mattress.

Or maybe San Diego is the mattress.

Or maybe the world is the mattress.

Chente run-jumping on the mattress-world with his bread-wine-glass.

Yes, this is how it is, and I am happy with that.

I am happier than I could ever imagine. Happy like a volcano blowing its top straight up in the air. Happy like a horse kicking its cruel owner in the face then running off and jumping over a thousand fences on its path to freedom.

Like that horse, I'm running happily, laughing happily because the mattress-world is awful and then sometimes it's not. Like, *suddenly* it's not. Like in brief moments as if the sun breaks through the clouds and casts this lovely golden beam right down on your lucky head. Your lucky head, which is usually your unlucky head, but now it's lucky and my *god* the light feels good. It feels so good you laugh. Like, haha, fuck you, world. Like, haha, I love you, world. Fuck you. I love you. I love you. Fuck you. Like that, haha.

Behind me the bouncer chasing us looks like a professional wrestler from Russia or maybe a professional wrestler in character as a dastardly, stern, militant '80s Soviet Russian, only he's in a tux and his bald skull is polished like a wax museum statue, like an egg you want to crack open and drop in a frying pan.

I'm lagging behind Chente, breathing so hard my sides are going to split, my heart jerking in my chest because I'm not much of a runner. I'm slower than Chente, but when I look back the bouncer is fading in view, and then he's stopped. Bent at the waist. Big hands on his knees. Catching his breath.

8

As I run, I scoop the last piece of fried, breaded eggplant and what's left of the mozzarella and red sauce off my plate. I shove it in my mouth then toss the plate up in the air as an act of celebration—up to the moon that looks just like it, up, up, spinning, hurtling up, up, up ...

SCRAMBLED EGGS,
OR THE INTRODUCTION TO THE STORY

****

In the 1996 film *Big Night,* the Italian brothers Primo, a chef, and Secondo, the manager of the restaurant they own together, are about to lose everything. This is the New Jersey Shore, 1950s. The brothers have emigrated from the Abruzzo region of Southern Italy in hopes of making a life for themselves in America—a life where they have their own restaurant, where they call the shots, and where they can rise as high as they want simply by putting in the work. Their restaurant is called the Paradise, and while Primo's food is visionary, and although he puts everything of himself into what he creates, he and Secondo are overshadowed by Pascal's, a neighboring restaurant, wildly popular despite its third-rate food.

Secondo, desperate to swim while he and Primo are clearly drowning, has decided to give it one last shot, and the brothers spend much of the film organizing a feast for the traveling Italian-American singer Louis Prima who is meant to stop in at the Paradise that night at the request of their rival Pascal. Though locked in ruthless competition with the Paradise, Pascal wants to give the boys a friendly leg-up. The viewer of the film (or the reader of Joseph Tropiano's excellent novel adaptation of the screenplay) will immediately see the danger here.

We are then brought into the preparation of the feast, the fried eggplant, the crostino, three types of risotto, the caponata, and then the course before the meat plates—a timpano, which is a gourmet all-in of ziti pasta, marinara sauce, sliced hardboiled eggs, meatballs, provolone, and salami, all baked together inside a great dome of pastry crust, then cut like thick slices of bread to reveal the strata of ingredients. The presentation is a beautiful thing—lavish, richly colorful, something a mythic hero might eat, or some gluttonous, epicurean lord in a Renaissance painting sitting at a great wooden table with a human skull, an hourglass, a gilded bird cage, and an open book set amongst the meal.

As the various guests and friends from the neighborhood assemble in anticipation of meeting the singer, they begin to drink the restaurant's wine and cocktails and try the appetizers and early courses. The mood is celebratory, light, and decadent (though respectable, likeable, working class). The hours tick by. As you might imagine, Louis Prima is nowhere to be seen.

There is a great line in the film that embodies a special type of ragged hope you see often in Americans—a breathless, earnest, tunnel vision optimism, of expectation and aspiration in the face of certain defeat. Secondo (played by a young and fiery Stanley Tucci), forever driving his brilliant but stubbornly idealistic brother, says to him (Primo, played by Tony Shalhoub), "After tonight, everything will be different."

This is a sentiment felt by countless dreamers on New Year's Eve or the night before turning 18 or 21. It's about having faith in restarts, a belief that one good action or element might set a faulty system right again, one brave act could restore the balance long knocked off-kilter.

"After tonight, everything will be different," says Secondo, and sitting at home alone with a laptop in front of you when the city is on lockdown and you haven't left the house in months or in the theater sipping your soda, holding that oversized bucket of popcorn on your lap, you believe him. You believe him even if the skeptical, cynical pessimist in you is sure the famous singer will never show. You believe him because if such things happen in *his* life, they can happen in yours as well. You can fix the broken pieces of the last few years. You can rise like we all hope to rise. You can ascend gloriously over the course of one star-kissed, magical night. One goddamn fucking outrageously important night. Maybe that's all you need. Maybe tonight is *your* night. Close your eyes. Let the room fall quiet. Listen to the wind rattling the window panes like invisible hands shaking them. Listen to the voice of the night, which is your voice after all, your *true* voice, the voice of your unaffected desires and purest hopes. (Or is it truth at all? Does it matter? Sometimes the key to getting what you want is the delusion it takes to get there.)

I have been at that place more times than I care to count—in the backseats of cars, at parties, alone in strange towns—and I know I will be there again. The fact that often all of this hoping and trying and earnestness leads to disappointment should stop me from believing, but it hasn't. Why not? Why keep patching the hull of a ship that will never float? Because that is who we are. That is the self-defeating burden of the American character, and it is also our greatest weapon. We, like Woody Guthrie wrote in his 1943 list of New Year's resolutions, keep that "hoping machine" running. What is a hoping machine? It's everything, the heart and sum of us, the grand totality of being human in this often hopeless, daunting, shitty life. As I write this in the second year of the COVID-19 pandemic, I'm still hoping. I'm hoping despite terrible odds and growing death tolls, a country burning, and a house divided. I'm still hoping.

As Secondo and Primo's guests devour the food, the night stretching toward dawn, you hold out hope along with the brothers. They trust that the singer will arrive and that he will love the meal and tell his famous friends about it, and because of his endorsement and influence the Paradise will thrive like Pascal's. In the film you love the brothers' hope and you love them for hoping, but you know it is a fight they will not win. You know because you have been *trained* to know. This is how life is. We try. We hope. We lose. We are disappointed and we accept disappointment with silent acquiescence. Sometimes our plans work out and all is well. Often, we fail. We are trained to accept that.

In the morning, the brothers lives lie in ruins. Louis Prima didn't show (he was never going to; it was a setup by the devilish Pascal). The brothers have emptied their bank account in preparation of the feast and their hopes were all for naught. They failed, and because they failed, they will lose the Paradise. Maybe Pascal is Satan and success is the apple of temptation and now the brothers (the first, Primo, Adam, the second, Secondo, Eve) will be driven from the Garden for striving beyond their station.

There is a beautiful scene at the end of the film involving eggs. At dawn, Secondo begins to prepare breakfast. The Puerto Rican waiter Cristiano (played by the singer Marc Anthony) is asleep on the butcher's block by the stove. Cristiano wakes up as Secondo busies himself with the task, and takes a seat on the block, clearly hungover. Secondo, though not a genius chef like his brother, cooks one of the most hypnotically natural and transcendent meals of the film (or of any film). It is a meal you know he has cooked for his brother and himself more times than he can count, and he moves through the steps seamlessly, gracefully, not like a dancer but like one who has been dancing all their life.

Secondo takes a small bowl of eggs to the low, flat stove in the middle of the room. He sets a pan on the burner, the flames rising high then dropping back again. With a practiced ease, he pours olive oil in the pan, cracks the eggs into another bowl, whisks the eggs for a quick few seconds, and adds a pinch of salt. Then he pours the eggs into the hot pan, stirring them, shaking the pan, flipping the eggs which are now one sheet of perfect yellow, and then it's done.

M.F.K. Fisher writes that to fry a good egg you must get in and get out. Touch the egg to the heat then pull it away as quickly as you are able. This is how Secondo cooks in the scene. The eggs touch the pan, and before you know they are lifted away—done, complete.

We are given in those silent moments a love letter to cooking and to food and to the ritual of eating in fellowship. There are a few very brief lines of dialogue in the scene, all between the waiter Cristiano and Secondo, and all as the scene opens. For the bulk of the film's final minutes there is no dialogue.

Secondo divides the meal into thirds using the spatula, serving Cristiano and himself and leaving the rest in the pan.

They eat. Secondo sitting at the table. Cristiano sitting on it, legs crossed at the ankles, both eating the eggs with torn-off hunks of leftover baguette from last night.

Then Primo walks into the room, disheveled, hungover too, and hesitant (over the course of the previous night, the brothers have fallen out spectacularly).

As Primo stands watching, Secondo gets up, takes a third plate from the rack, and sets a place for his brother at the table.

Without saying anything, Primo sits down at the table next to his brother—together again after a night of travails, celebration, and disillusionment. As Cristiano gets up and leaves the room to give the brothers space, Secondo drapes his left arm across his brother's shoulders and Primo wraps his right arm over Secondo's, and silently, they eat.

It is a perfect moment, emotionally rich without need for dialogue, heavy without succumbing to hopelessness, hopeful without being blind or cheap or unrealistic. In that moment you know it will be okay. Maybe just for now, for today. The relief in that final scene is rapturous, beautiful, and dazzlingly incandescent. It is hope like a lantern light, like a bell in the fog. Together Secondo and Primo will pick up the pieces. They will live, and they will tackle what's set out for them.

After the Fall is where the story truly begins, doesn't it? The Garden is just a prelude, an introduction for what is to come—and what's to come is everything, the chaos and joy of life on this planet, reality, this, me, you, our lives, our dreams, our history, our future, the pain of birth, the pain of life, the pain of love, of work, of that endless striving, striving, striving, of hope, aspiration, expectation, optimism, belief that it will work out, trust that you will be cared for, anticipation of good times, and excitement for what may come. We are born sweet and soft and desirous of kind moments and thrilling heights, but what do we get? The good and the bad. The rough and the kind. The greatest days and the ugliest nights. We are babies shoved into the storm, made to watch as the world goes through the wildest upheavals. We stand up and we walk and we grow as shit rains down upon us. Maybe we experience perfection. In the small hours. In surprise doses. Maybe we get the best of what life is, if only for the tiniest, fleeting second.

After tonight, everything will be different because it is always different, each new dawning day. Whether for good or ill, our world is forever changing. You plan for the bad (or you ignore it) and you hope like hell for the good. Life is a gift, and it's also a curse. It's a trap, a ripening piece of fruit with worms at the heart of it, a lovely sunset, a poisoned cup of wine offered by the one you love most, a feast you will carry with you and remember until you are old or until your memories begin to weather, fade, and sift away like dry sand. Life is held aloft by moments where you are coasting on pure belief, on hope, on a wish, and it is smashed down repeatedly as you fight to keep standing.

After tonight, everything will be different, and we work and we hope and we put our back into it even if "it" is a stone wall that will never budge. After tonight, everything will be different, and we keep believing because we've seen it happen. We have watched the miraculous levitation of others. We have witnessed the beauty of moving beyond the shitty, foul, sad hours all humans trudge through. After tonight, everything will be different. Because it will, whether that difference is sweet or bitter, and we will wake up and we will sit down at the breakfast table and we will eat.

CACTUS CANDY

CACTUS CANDY

Now I am starting at the beginning and moving chronologically to tell how it was to live when I lived and what life was once like and will never be again—never again because life is forever becoming a new thing. Sometimes this is good. Sometimes catastrophically bad in a way that feels like the good world is gone, and that the shit world is here to stay. The shit world rising above you like the tail of a giant scorpion in a Greek myth. The shit world like granite boulders falling on your house from the highest shit mountain. The shit world will devastate you, consume you, grind you up like grain until you are unrecognizable. The way we live, our culture, our society will evolve just as animals do. Only a culture does it faster. As a mass, our culture and the fabric of who we are will gallop madly forward, racing at breakneck speed, changing with the new terrain, hanging just above the tempest and squall, adapting in order to thrive. Failing too, but what survives is what we move within, and what was before will never be again. The good world is always here. All you need to do is change in the right way, find the right streets, knock on the right doors. Mostly this is impossible, and the shit world remains.

In Mexico, when I am three, my family goes to the icehouse. This is a stone wall carved out from the side of a mountain in the jungle. There are holes in the stone. Long ago someone cut deep rectangles out from the wall, rectangles the shape and size you might slide a coffin into, but in those spaces are blocks of ice packed in jungle leaves.

You pay a woman for the ice then a man with a small monkey on his shoulder helps you out. (The monkey's face is a shock of white with shining black eyes that stare at you steadily as if sizing you up.) The man loads the ice blocks into our light blue Volkswagen bus while we stand to the side, waiting.

In what I believe to be my earliest memory, as we

wait for the man to come out of the jungle and assist us, I am told by my mother that we will eat cactus candy on the drive back to the coast, and while I remember the slurring humidity of the jungle, the sweat dripping off us, and our clothes sticking to our bodies, and the beat-up Volkswagen bus and everyone with long hair to their waist and the men with beards and mustaches, I don't remember getting or eating cactus candy.

I have however kept the smell—somewhere between mango and apricot. It is a scent I have smelled many times over the years, whether in the form of candy lip gloss I tried on as a teenager, or cheap air freshener, or in soap or shampoo or conditioner. Last week it came to me at Costco. Standing at the sink in the restroom washing my hands next to a row of shoppers in their pandemic masks. It arrived in a rush. Vivid, potent, intact. I stared at my face in the mirror (masked, tired, an adult) and I *remembered*.

The smell brings back standing next to my impossibly tall uncle Lenn in front of the icehouse, and it brings the moment back in rich, bold colors (mustard yellow striping on green jungle leaves so dark they're nearly black) and adjoining scents (mud, decay, gasoline, cigarette smoke). The candy is gone but so much more remains.

We learn early that smell is one of the best triggers to memory. It sweeps you up with it like a great, surging tide, and it takes you somewhere you've been before. Often, you are unable to see where you were, or what happened in that place, or what you were thinking, but you are *there*, firmly rooted—if fleetingly, transient. You are set down in a cross-section of the past and you live in it vibrantly for a bright, hot flash of seconds and then it is pulled from you (or lifted off like steam). It is a momentary variation of reality, strong yet impermanent.

Sense can be time travel in a way that conscious memory or imagination cannot. Driven by our senses and the memories they bring, we are connected to all threads of our time like the strings of a vast harp playing gently before us, a harp that bends circular like the universe, returning to where it began. We are connected to everyone we knew and all of the places we went and all of the stories we have been told. We are tied to our past even if we try to escape it, even if we strain against those bonds until we wreck the present in dire and frightful ways.

Of course you can't live in the past or it will serve as a sort of opiate, clouding your perception and squandering (or perhaps dissipating) your strength. You must engage actively in the moment at hand. Life ends in death and there is no stopping your march toward it. So, you pick up the coins you find scattered along the paths of the shit world and you look for more rather than dwelling upon the ones you have spent or lost. You fix your gaze to the road ahead of you and you keep walking as you remember the place you came from and what you saw while you were there.

LOBSTER

Sometimes when you're young enough you forget that the place you are in is not your home. Something like, I have been here longer than I can remember and because of that this is where I live.

We have been in Mexico longer than I understand because I am three and my past is amorphous. My past and time are like the details of a valley (and a town in the valley) as seen through fog.

Only the present moment makes sense to me, and in the present everyone is deathly sick from eating spoiled shrimp except for me and my cousins Stella and Jean Claude.

I remember the hospital room in the jungle.

The priest in his black robes knelt next to my uncle, reading his last rights.

The courtyard of the hospital with its palm trees and the nuns hurrying along the hall between the rooms.

Monkeys in the trees—moving like black spiders or cats against the hot silver disc of jungle sun.

A church bell tolling somewhere—slow, languid in the heat.

The nuns talk to us in Spanish, mostly soft and gentle, sometimes shouting, urgent.

We don't understand a word.

My cousins are older. Jean Claude, eight, Stella, seven. The adults in our family (our protectors) are dying in a foreign country while Jean Claude, Stella, and I sit in the hot grass under the palm trees, eating chunks of mango from a blue plastic bowl like the kind you put popcorn in.

The hospital is full of death.

We see bodies carried out.

Bodies under white sheets.

Or bodies on full display, mouths open, arms spread wide.

It's full of life too. Babies born. Happy families crowding into the doorless adobe rooms that line the courtyard.

Our parents survive, but we are waylaid for what feels like months in the jungle before they are able to leave the hospital. At some point we get back in the Volkswagen bus and drive to the coast, after which memory pays even less attention to chronology.

Memories of the rest, also some of my first: lying on the front of a surfboard as my mother paddles it up the dark, narrow canyon of a mangrove swamp at dusk, and the jungle birds lifting from the trees in slow white flocks. We stop and she sits up on the board and pulls a gray, rotting fishing net from the black water, saying, "James. Look what I found." Then: a tiny black octopus from the net writhing in the palm of her hand, its many arms twisting and turning, its *body* twisting and turning, moving like a screw.

Then: sitting on a towel on a bright gray sand beach, and a friend of the family walking up the shore, his long hair slicked-back wet, carrying a short surfboard the shape of a pumpkin seed under his arm. The surfboard is red and it has a logo the shape of a lightning bolt down its center and his knee is split open from the coral. Blood runs thick down the dark skin of his leg, leaving a wet trail in the sand. When he gets close you can see the gleaming white bone as red blood pumps around it.

Then: a cliffside and the metallic gray sea below— the tails and spiny heads of lobsters scattered across the weedy cliff face where people threw them after they ate dinner. (Some of them are ours.)

The taste of the lobster (the memory) is gone, but what remains is the smell of clarified butter; the dirty steam of the boiling pot of water on the camp stove; the sharp crackling sound as the lobster's body is ripped in two. The tail dropped in the steaming pot. The head cast aside. (The *horror* of that, of death, of yourself torn in two while your body still lives. Into the boiling water you're dropped. A pot lid set over the back half of you as the front half lies struggling on the hardpacked dirt, watching yourself boil until the life fades from your eyes.)

Later: the same beach, the smell of campfire smoke, the sea like a sheet of aluminum foil below the cliff. I'm sitting in the tent I share with my parents, holding a goat's skull I found in the desert, and in the morning the tent's stitched seams are traced in lines of ants and the skull swarms black as they eat what's left of the flesh.

Later: a terrible stink in the air as we drive through the desert and when we get close it's a mountain of dead sharks on the side of the road as high as the bus. Thousands of them piled together, dried in the sun, their bodies twisted in death.

Then: a desert town at dusk, and we're driving slow through it (through the bruise-purple dusk, and through the town), driving past a wedding at a mission-arched, adobe church. The bride in a pale lilac gown and the groom in all gray with white *charro* piping and a silver-banded cowboy hat, arm in arm, walking down the steps through the crowd, waving at the people, laughing, happy.

Driving: a graveyard in the desert. In the distance, a group of mourners in black standing around (and above) a new grave. The tombstones irregular across the hilly landscape behind them, bristling, tall and squat and sharp and smooth, rising and falling in height like the buildings and towers of a city.

Then: the glare of sunshine through the bus windows, the turquoise bead crucifix hung from the rearview mirror swinging side to side, and the smell of coconut surf wax melting.

Over the road noise and the rumble of the Volkswagen bus, Elton John sings through the speakers, "goodbyyyye doesn't mean this has to be the end."

He's right, you know? It doesn't have to be. There's only one true end for you. You never know the things you're going to see.

Close your eyes for a few seconds then open them again.

Keep them open.

Are they open?

Say "Yes," if they are.

I mean, really, *say* it.

Say it out loud.
Say "Yes." Say it with me. "Yes."
Look up from the pages of this book.
Look at the world around you.
Now, what do you see?

TUNA MELT

****

My first memories after Mexico are of my parents' sea-food restaurant—the dark wood booths, the gray San Diego sky darkening outside the windows, the stripmall parking lot, the noisy kitchen with oil flashing to a pillar of fire from the pan. The walls lined with aquariums of tropical fish, and at night the blue glow of the aquariums and the red glass candles on the table are the only light in the place. The chef makes my meals because we are living in a 1976 Dodge Brougham motorhome on a back street behind the Balboa Avenue stripmall as my parents' business fails progressively. This means we live in the restaurant and we eat in the restaurant and (speaking for myself, on late afternoons just back from preschool) we (I) sleep in the restaurant's dark back-room office while my mother sits at a desk keeping the books with an adding machine and a stack of receipts.

I have no distinct memory of the chef or of the cooks, but I remember sourdough bread in long thin slices cut from a round. The bread is buttered lightly then seared on the grill until there are rough black lines scorched across it, and then the sandwich is made—tuna salad with mayo and flecks of pickle, a slice of cheddar, no celery please, after which it is placed in the oven just briefly to melt the cheese. (There is nothing like but-tered, grilled sourdough bread. Sourdough bread is good and butter is good but sourdough that has been buttered then grilled? It's a gift of perfect chemistry as if butter and sourdough bread are the greatest friends of all time and would rather spend every moment to-gether than do anything else. Friends who are maybe in love but a love that never ruins the friendship. Friends who are two halves of the same person. Friends who are obsessed with each other but in a healthy way. Friends who don't need to be friends but are friends because they *want* to be.) This is my breakfast, lunch, and din-ner with a glass of milk and a hot basket of steak fries on the side (a lemon slice to squeeze on the fries which are seasoned with salt and pepper). My parents are going through hell keeping the restaurant together. I see none of this.

There is a lovely joy you might experience a few times (if at all, and only if you are very lucky) when your parents are a castle wall keeping the worst of the world from you. This is before you learn about the realities of war and hate and genocide, of bills you must pay and jobs you have to work, about bullies, violence, before you are told you must debase yourself to even the lowest forms of authority, and that not everyone wants the best for you—that some will think nothing of shooting up your school and killing your friends, that often the world of humanity is a barbarous, vile, stupid place.

If your parents can keep that from you (at least during those first few years) it is a sustaining action that will allow you to grow without the many stresses and abject horror of being human. (That will come later, but if it is held back from you for even the shortest while, you will better handle it when it arrives.)

For now, you can be four years old with little blue shorts and a stained t-shirt with an iron-on image of Shamu on it, and you can eat a perfect tuna melt with fries three times a day, and you can stare at the world with open eyes—loving butter and sourdough, loving the eucalyptus trees in the stripmall as the wind blows their branches in the summer, loving the pale blue sky, the wild mysteries of life, the magic you still believe in, the people, your friends, your family, the animals you meet, the future you have waiting for you.

Later you will be hurt. You will learn that your beautiful life is a cruel life too. For now, you can walk unimpeded through the halls of your realm, loving and excited and earnest, knowing nothing but long sweet days that feel as if they will never end.

KRAFT *De Luxe* **SLICES**

8 SLICES

PASTEURIZED PROCESS AMERICAN CHEESE

PIMENTO
BRICK
SWISS
OLD ENGLISH

Easy
as peeling
a banana..."

t's how easy it is to separate the perfect Kraft
xe Slices.

, some people think we should have given these
a name like "Easy-snaks" or "Handi-cheez" or
ond Treat."

nly they <u>are</u> the easiest, quickest way in the
to swell-eating cheese sandwiches. But that

your life ... in <u>any</u> sliced cheese.

This new method not only mak
separate easily and keep beauti
flavor. (You'll find this the
cheese you've ever had!) And th
cleanliness because the slices a
pasteurization; sealed within sec

AMERICAN CHEESE

****

When my parents lose their restaurant, the bank takes everything except the motorhome and our station wagon. We live in the motorhome in parking lots, and we live outside the houses of my parents' friends in Pacific Beach until the neighbors call the police. For months we live in a parking lot on an island in the middle of the bay surrounded by grassy parks and a resort gone to seed. The island is connected on either side to the mainland by the great arcing causeway of commuter bridges that link Pacific Beach to Point Loma, Ocean Beach, and the Sports Arena. In the center, on the island, where the two bridges meet, we park the motorhome in a lot with a patchy crabgrass park and rusty barbeque rings and a rocky shore and beyond that the bay, which is a nice thing to wake up to and see—the pink light of dawn on the baywaters or the big coastal sunsets with the dusky colors of amaranth and yellow carnation, of cherry fruit punch so red you can taste it. So red you want to stab a straw into the skyline and drink it.

For a while we live at Campland, a trailerpark down by the bay. In the early 1980s it is a rough place where cars are stolen in the middle of the day, trailers are looted while the families are off at school and work, and the windows of doublewides shot out. It is also beautiful, and that is what I remember.

Campland sat (and still sits, though it is no longer rough) on the shore of a saltwater marsh in Mission Bay. It is bordered by Rose Creek, a golf course, and the sports fields of the high school I would end up at a decade later. The marsh is lovely with its ripe, dark, comforting muddy salt smell and the tiny, colorful crabs massing on the barnacled pilings and sunning themselves on the wet rocks. I remember the sand pipers stepping cautious through the shallows looking for fish and I remember the silence of the marsh—a pure, breathless, crystalline silence where each sound is clear and distinct and rendered in hard edges as if cut from stone.

Later, when Campland gets too violent for us, we move to the Santa Fe Trailerpark in Rose Canyon next to the freeway. I remember the musky, sharp smell of maple leaves in the fall and the creaking of the tree branches in the wind. The easy days sitting in the back of the motorhome watching *Mister Rogers' Neighborhood* on PBS with the big curved glass windows behind and above me, the overcast skies gray and featureless. In these memories it is always autumn, somewhere in the days or weeks before Halloween, and there is a sweet joy in knowing the holidays are coming soon, waiting triumphant and expectant for you like grandparents who love you more than anything, waiting courageously in the near future. It's the joy of Halloween, Thanksgiving, Christmas, and New Year's Eve with its wonderful pile-up of orange construction paper jack o' lanterns taped to the windows with toothy smiles, stuffing and gravy steaming on your plate as you reach for a crescent roll in a basket that feels miles away from where you sit, the shimmering tinsel like a waterfall, the wonderous thrill of expecting Santa Claus, red and green and blue string lights from Mervyn's fading gently before rising to a glow again, the *Charlie Brown Christmas* special with its soft, snowy jazz drums as the characters ice skate, and you're staying up later than you ever have on the last day of the year, then the countdown to midnight.

My strongest memory of living at the freeway trailerpark is of being very hungry at night, my father off working to start a new business (the windows of the motorhome black, depthless, an inky void as I climb down from my carpeted bedroom loft above the cab), then opening the fridge to find it completely empty except for a single slice of American cheese sitting alone on the bare white racks. I remember the light of the refrigerator—clean, white, clear, blinding, as if staring into the cabin of some futuristic spacecraft.

Many years later, sitting on a beautiful, uncomfortable, gold-thread couch at a party in Topanga Canyon, I talk with or rather am talked at by a Frenchman my age, a friend (I assume) of the famous folksinger who owns the opulent, gaudy mansion where I'm staying for the weekend. I am in the middle of a book tour. The Frenchman doesn't know this, and I have no plans to tell him. (One of the quickest ways to bring out the most obnoxious and awkward tendencies in people is to say you write books. Mention you're on a book tour and you're doomed.)

The Frenchman has a bag of cocaine the size of a smashed plum. Every few minutes he leans over the glass coffeetable at our knees and snorts a line, scowls, rubbing the bridge of his nose, then continues to talk. He wears a ratty fishermen's sweater in gray wool like the famous photo of Hemingway and his brown hair is carefully untidy.

"Ameri*cains*," he says. "Your cheese it is *sheet*."

I tell the Frenchman he is not wrong. American cheese truly is shit, but (I make sure to point out) American cheese is not my cheese. My new friend, who isn't my friend at all (or perhaps anyone else's here because he won't leave my side), cuts me off midsentence to tell me how the only thing worse than American cheese is American bread.

I agree with him, disavowing American bread. Though I am not entirely sure which bread he is referring to. I imagine Wonder Bread, white bread.

The truth is for a very long time American cheese *was* my cheese and Wonder Bread was the finest thing in the motorhome's pantry.

That night in the motorhome with the lovely slice of cheese in the fridge I feel nothing bad. It doesn't scare or disappoint me. I peel the plastic off the slice and eat it then go back to whatever I was doing before.

My perception of the economic state of my family is saved or perhaps shielded by my parents. I am unaware that we are profoundly, desperately poor. My parents do not let on or complain about money in my presence, which is to say life in the various trailerparks we stay at is sweet, quiet, and safe. I move about my world joyfully, half in a dream, half grounded by the fantastic and alluring world around me. The marsh birds. The crumbling ruins of parking lots. The bayshore. The Mexican families fishing from the rocks under the bridge on the island. The Ford Rancheros and El Caminos without wheels up on cinderblocks or under blue tarps and the Buicks and T-Birds with blown-out front windshields or hanging bumpers parked next to doublewides and decommissioned school buses, their windows taped-up with newspapers. The men in the trailerparks where we live are shirtless with tattoos on their shoulders and scraggly mullets or rat tails. The women sit in pairs on trailer steps smoking cigarettes and drinking sodas or beer and staring at me as I walk past in the dusk. The kids my age are just like any kids anywhere and we care about nothing but playing. Or rather I care about nothing. Whether the parents of the children I play with buffer them from the harsher realities of living very poor in America I cannot say. I did not have the perspective then and now all is lost to time, unreachable.

My parents' finances crash to wild depths and rise victoriously then fall again, and this is how we live for years.

American cheese is a constant and loyal companion. Melted over eggs on English muffins. With Buddig turkey slices and mayo on pita bread. Eternally grilled on sourdough. A slice of cheese smeared with peanut butter then folded like a taco. Smeared with mayo then folded like a taco. Smeared with strawberry jam then folded like a taco.

The cheese taco in all its incarnations is not a good thing in retrospect, but at the time, at that very particular moment of childhood, the fact remains that I don't know what "good" is and haven't yet questioned good in contrast to bad, so perhaps that in itself makes it good. Perhaps it's good enough to believe that something is good. If you believe a thing to be what it is most definitely *not*, does that in turn make it what you want it to be, in essence making it what it is not? Is a thing's worth determined by accepted standards of quality and popular taste or is it determined by love? Someone's favorite film is still their favorite film regardless of whether someone else might consider it to be shit. A second and differing opinion does not stop the film from being someone's (*anyone's*) favorite. Even if it were only one person's favorite film, it is because of this a "favorite film," irrespective of criticism, and by way of that it is a thing of value.

The American cheese taco in all its varieties, styles, and permutations—with peanut butter, with mayo, with jam—it exists. This is an irrefutable fact, and most (if not all) things that exist have someone or many someones who sincerely love them in a very fundamental, crucial, integral way. To which we may conclude, the American cheese taco is loved.

I think of this often—how ~~~~ breakingly shitty life can be but the fact tha~~~~ ~~~~oved can make it feel less so. Not *loving ~~~~ ~~~~, per se*, because that's different, but knowing that people love things, knowing that people care about even the smallest, stupidest things enough to love them can give you hope in humanity. Because maybe if people love something they can't be so bad. Maybe if they feel and know love they can change, they can redeem themselves. If you can feel love for something as gross, base, and undesirable as a folded slice of American cheese made into a taco with peanut butter, maybe you can learn to love your neighbor and the Earth enough to take a position of stewardship, to save and not ravage, to remedy and not destroy. That I hate so many people and love so few is a thing I'm at odds with, a problem I want desperately to fix. Will I? Probably not. I'm prone to being gloomy, judgmental, and pessimistic, and try as I might, I cannot change that. Still, this much I know: it is better to be surprised by your unexpected victories than disappointed by the losses you neglected to predict.

Humanity is a monster that will eat you alive. It is a pestilence sweeping across the landscape. But people? People can be alright. Loving even the smallest number of people is a reason to stick around, a reason to get out of bed in the morning. Trying to love people while holding onto hope is a daily war where the enemy is so much stronger than you. The enemy has tanks and bombs.

They have napalm they'll drop on you, and you've got Nerf guns and wooden swords. It's disheartening even on the best days. So you look for reasons, for evidence as to why you should keep trying. Is the fact that people love the American cheese taco evidence of humanity's potential for goodness? Is it a reason to believe in something better? Today it is. In this moment it is.

FISH TACOS

****

In fourth grade my parents take me out of school. We cross the US/Mexico border and drive down to a beach in Baja California where the way in is a narrow, rocky canyon prone to flashfloods, a rough three-hour drive over ruts and around sharp bends, and finally to the sandy desert lowlands that lead to a wide, flat, wind-swept beach set in a cove nestled into the hills; a vast, stormy, dark blue sea in front of us stretching to the horizon. My class assignment is to keep a diary of our time in Mexico.

The daily entries are brief:

"Today I played on the beach."

"I played with my Gobots in the back of the truck. Leader-1's arm broke off."

"I ran around."

"I ate Chicken and Stars soup and loved it!"

"I found a dead crab."

Mostly I explore the beach and the desert behind our camp. In the cliffs overlooking the sea there are caves used as shrines by the local fishermen to pray for luck and safety before going to sea. The caves are small, dry, and clean, and in the nooks of the rock are set votive candles, seashells, *peso* coins, and the beautiful gold-plate tin icons of Catholic saints. I sit in the prayer caves and watch the beach so far below—my father's white truck like a toy car and the black speck of our dog running across the coastal plain of gray. The sea is dark blue and blown to white caps of chop by the wind, and it's cold—colder than back home, the breeze whipping eastward across the ocean all day and blowing hard at night. We cook our food over a fire, and we wash our plates and pots with handfuls of sand and a piece of brown kelp as a scrubber in the tidepools, and we sleep under a pile of old quilts and blankets in the back of the truck. All night the coyotes howl. It's a terrible, frantic, yipping shriek. When they come into our camp after dark and root through the things we've left out, our coward dog pretends to sleep.

The days are chilly and gray. We keep a small fire burning in a ring of rocks, the wind beating the flame long and flat, the musky, sour smell of ash and smoke in the air. I spend my time reading *The Book of Three* up in the prayer caves or walking alone on the beach or standing ankle-deep in the cold water as the tide pours in—staring out to sea, staring at the tiny, indistinct dots of fishing boats, wondering if the men on them are the same ones who use the caves.

The Book of Three is part of a series of children's fantasy novels I've brought with me. I keep *The Black Cauldron*, *The Castle of Llyr*, *Taran Wanderer*, and *The High King* tucked away under the front seat of the truck. I lose myself in the adventures of Taran Assistant Pig-Keeper and the evil deeds of the Horned-King and Arawn Death-Lord of Annuvin. I read, "Most of us are called on to perform tasks far beyond what we can do. Our capabilities seldom match our aspirations, and we are often woefully unprepared." I have to ask my mother what "woefully" and "aspirations" are, and she explains each word patiently. I read, "Do you not believe that animals know grief and fear and pain? The world of men is not an easy one for them," and I think of my dog, and I understand.

When our food begins to run out, we live off fish my father brings in by net or by line. Some days a small wooden boat of local fishermen comes to shore, and they trade lobsters or crabs for shotgun shells and jugs of fresh water. The men look like explorers from another time. They are burned dark by the sun and they laugh easily and sometimes they try to talk to me, and my mother translates. I love them. They are heroic, alive, and something to aspire to. (Aspire. Aspirations.)

The days pass until I lose track of the calendar, until there is no week or weekend, just a long procession of morning, afternoon, evening, night—of sun, wind, and sea.

My school diary entries document the small details:

"Today we ate fish my dad caught. I found some bones in the desert. I said are these people's bones and my mom said no they are a coyote's bones, but I think they're actually human bones and I think my mom doesn't want me to be scared."

"Today we had lobster from the fishermen. I finished *The Book of Three.*"

"A dead seal washed up on the beach and we buried it because of the smell. My dad said a fisherman must have shot it."

"Today we had crab meat in our spaghetti and I didn't like it."

"I saw a plane fly overhead. It was very small."

"We're out of salt."

"I played in the desert and saw a black cat watching me. I love the cat. I want to name it."

"One of my teeth is loose and it hurts. I saw the cat again today. I named him Gurgi."

"I tried to find Gurgi and I found a shack in the desert. It's full of huge whale bones. They're ribs my mom says."

"My tooth is gone. I swallowed it while I was sleeping. I haven't seen Gurgi for three days."

One morning after we have lived at the beach for what feels like years, a man rides a horse up the shore toward our camp.

We see him coming from far away. My mother stops cooking breakfast and my father stands up from his lawn chair, shielding his eyes from the gray light, watching.

"I should get my gun," he says.

"Shush," my mother says.

We're dressed in ski jackets and long pants and wool hats. I have on two pairs of sweatpants and a thick coat and my father's old sunglasses that fit over my face like a black shield. My mother wears a scarf and an old, ratty quilted snow vest over her purple sweatshirt. A brisk, hard wind flaps our sleeves and the legs of our pants, and seeps into the gaps of our clothing.

I've had a cold all week.

"Woefully bad," is the way I describe it in my school diary using one of my new words.

I'm ready to go home, but we stay.

Sometimes I wonder if we're running away from something. (I know my father has an enemy and that when he talks about him, he goes into a fury and says he's going to shoot him, but I don't know anything beyond the man's name.)

The harder gusts carry sand with them, sand that speckles you like snow or hail, that gets in your eyes and into your hair.

It feels as if it takes hours for the man on the horse to arrive.

When he does, he lifts a hand in greeting and says, "*Buenos días,*" good morning, and my mother answers with the same, then he sits for a while watching us.

The horse is tall and strong and dark red, and the man is dressed in brown waterproof pants that look expensive, the sturdy black rubber boots you wear on a boat, and a yellow rain slicker. He has curly black hair, and it blows around his face as he sits watching us, unsmiling, eyes narrow. He wears a leather strap diagonally across his chest and tucked behind his back is a rifle.

My mother asks him if he wants coffee. "*Quiere café?*"

The man makes a swiping motion in front of him with one hand as a no then tells us in English that a storm is coming. He says if the canyon floods it will be impossible to leave for weeks, perhaps months, and that if we are planning to leave any time soon we must go now. He points out to sea at the darkening clouds. "*Mira.* Is big one. Is very dangerous for you."

My mother says, "*Cuando,*" when. When is the storm coming?

"*Ahora mismo.* Is coming now. *Dos horas, más o menos,*" he says, tapping his wrist with a finger. Right now. Two hours, more or less.

"*Gracias. Nos vamos,*" says my mother, thanking him, telling him we are going to leave.

"*Pues, adios, buena suerte,*" says the man, telling us goodbye, good luck. He hits the heels of his boots against the horse's flank and shouts, "Yah!"

His horse turns and he rides away from us, kicking

up sand, moving fast and direct. Beautiful.

We pack quickly. My dad puts the dog in the back of the truck, and we leave just as the storm hits. On the drive through the canyon, the truck slides in the mud and spins out, colliding with the side of the rocky wall, a deafening bang and crunch. The truck is old and has trouble with the incline, its engine screaming wildly, while my father leans forward in his seat, eyes fixed on the road in front of us as water runs down the side of the canyon walls.

"Water's up to the tires," my mother says, looking out her window.

"I know," my father says under his breath. "We're going."

The truck struggles, fights to stay straight. A few miles down the line we lose traction and slide backward and my mother screams like we're in a horror movie. We spin out, and we fishtail again and again, then it's over. The road levels out into hardpacked dirt flats, and soon we're leaving the canyon walls behind.

We take a left and hit the smooth blacktop of the highway which feels like nothing, like coasting on air, and then we are driving north through the desert, silent, the air conditioner blowing.

The sky is pale blue and cloudless.

I settle in my seat in the back and open *The Black Cauldron* to its marked spot.

"Coulda been bad," my mother says.

"Spice-a life," my dad replies.

I read: "Is there not glory enough in living the days given to us?"

We celebrate getting out with dinner at a roadside restaurant on the tall, rocky cliffs near a beach where we plan to sleep for the night. The place is packed with adults my parents' age and groups of men dressed like the fishermen from our cove. They're laughing and talking loud and drinking beer while rowdy, exuberant *mariachi* music blares over the speakers. Kids run in and out of the place, and a tired-looking waitress steps around them as she brings armloads of plates to the tables. *This is how life should be*, is what my brain tells me in no particular words. What I see is a packed, crowded, busy, celebratory life—a life I want to live.

It's night now and the ocean as seen from our table by the window is calm and lit by a gray-dented white moon that hangs low over the horizon, casting its long, warbling reflection across the dark water.

We order fish tacos—beer battered pieces of fish, round like walnuts or in knotty clumps like chunks of ginger root, wrapped in corn tortillas with shredded cabbage, diced tomato, cilantro, and a white sauce poured across it all.

The white sauce is what I like best. It tastes like mayonnaise with vinegar and lime and something smoky along with that. It is a glorious thing—a sauce you could eat every day and on everything, but with the fish it's perfect. After weeks of eating seafood cooked over a fire with no salt and nothing on the side once our food ran out, this is as good as a meal can be. It feels more like a gift than a meal. Like a symphony, a standing ovation, and a glorious encore after sitting in the dark theater waiting. (Years later I will make the same tacos with breaded, deep-fried pieces of cauliflower instead of fish. The sauce I make is Vegenaise mayo, both lime zest and lime juice, salt, the smallest shake of black pepper, chipotle, and garlic powder.)

When we're done eating, the tired waitress comes to our table and brings us three more Cokes in tall glass bottles.

"You okay? Is good everything?"

My father says it was great and asks what kind of fish it was.

"Ohhh, you have to ask my hosbind. He catched them fresh today. I have not tried to eat just yet. I got too much work. Too much business," she says, then laughs, looking around the room, before saying, "Is worst problems to have, no?" She has a nice laugh, a smart person's laugh, a contained, gentle laugh that's honest and weary.

My mother agrees with the waitress and tells her that we had a restaurant in San Diego and that there were always problems.

The waitress laughs again and shakes her head. "Yeaaah," she says sadly, "every day something new. Is so much stress. *Dios Mío*. What happen your restaurant?"

My father tells her it went bankrupt

"Oh, sorry. Is no good. That is, you know, uh, my worse nightmare of all."

My mother asks the tired waitress if she runs the place.

"It's, uh, how you say, I *own* it. Is my business. Is stressful but ... no problem. I handle it. I like to be the boss. Not answer to no one. I like to, uh, rule my world. Be like *un rey* ... you know, a king."

My father says that's the dream.

"Yes, is the dream," she says, nodding, tired.

We ask for another plate of tacos and she goes back to the kitchen to put the order in.

The second round is even better than the first and there's more sauce this time. The corn tortillas are soft, but what's in the tacos is crunchy—the battered fish, the crisp shreds of cabbage. I squeeze a slice of lime into mine like my mother does and all is well in the world. I have no worries or fears or concerns. Just hopes, things I expect and want. My parents are young, and they keep me safe and the things we do are wonderful and new.

Life is about to change, and I have no idea. I'm a terrible idiot. The kind of idiot we all are for a while.

Which is the best thing to be.

Younger.

A kid.

A great, happy, terrible idiot living a dream of a life. What a thing to lose. But we move forward, pushed gently sometimes, other times not so. Moving, changing. Great, terrible, happy idiot babies become sad adults. But not yet. Before that, middle school.

GARLIC FISH PLATE

****

Glory be to the garlic fish plate at Los Panchos in Pacific Beach and evenings after a long awful day in middle school—tortured and hated, spat upon, hit in the stomach, smashed up against the handball wall, pantsed in front of the class while solving a math problem on the chalkboard, stolen from, laughed at, tripped, called a fag and ugly and retarded—the first thoughts of suicide blooming like some diseased orchid in a dark room. The desire to wipe myself clean from the map. To rub out my short history until the pink eraser at the end of the yellow pencil is dust upon the page. (O' to be dust, to be the lucky eraser that leaves the pencil behind.) Glory be to the tolling of the final school bell of the day and the sharp clang of locker doors slamming and the bustling, murmuring noise of the crowded hall as it empties out, then walking home alone in the pale afternoon sun of 1989. Glory be to a breaded filet of cod fried in garlic, olive oil, and butter, the fish neighboring a pile of Mexican rice, steam rising from it, three slices of bright green avocado, gorgeous refried beans topped with an oily puddle of orange cheddar marbled bright with monterey jack like the greatest lake you'd ever want to drown in. Glory be to the all-important stack of steamed corn tortillas wrapped in tinfoil in a plastic warmer the color of raspberry yogurt. Glory be. Glory *be*. The waiter Julio who looks like a Mexican president sets our plates down, and says, "You guys got everything? This look okay?" and we nod and maybe we say sure or great or this is perfect, and he says, "Alright, you just let me know if you need anything." My mother asks for more sour cream and Julio the Mexican president waiter says, "You got it! For just you or the whole table?" and my mother says, "For everybody please," and he says, "I'll bring you out so much sour cream it'll make the table collapse," and my heart swells and I love Los Panchos and the president waiter Julio and the possibility of endless sour cream. Glory be. To drink a Coke with a maraschino cherry and get refills while my parents sit across from me eating the same meal and talking happily about their seafood processing business, which has now begun to thrive. Glory be. We are middle class now. Glory be. We won't always be, but we are at this moment and glory be to that.

THE WORLD
TRADE CENTER
NEW YORK

NACHO CHEESE DORITOS

****

In 8th grade our class takes an end-of-year trip to the East Coast. The San Diego Unified School District calls it the "Washington Trip" and the Washington Trip begins in Virginia at Colonial Williamsburg and ends with a weekend in New York City after stopovers in D.C. and Boston. The Washington Trip is absolute shit and I hate it. I hate Paul Revere's narrow, cramped, awful house and I hate the Thomas Jefferson Memorial. I hate the Bunker Hill Monument and the JFK Library. I hate Tudor Place and I hate the White House. I hate the Pentagon and I hate the teachers and the parents who came along to chaperone and how they go out drinking every night once we're put up in our hotel rooms and bicker at us in the morning and smell like cigarettes and overripe fruit. The hotels are okay. I don't hate the hotels, but I hate the Tomb of the Unknown Soldier, the Capitol, the Washington Monument, and the buses they herd us onto and off of. I hate all my classmates who also hate me. I hate my classmates the way seals hate sharks. I want to be home sitting in my room. Reading comics. Reading magazines and books. Listening to tapes and records. In bed staying up late watching reruns of *Diff'rent Strokes* or Nick at Nite with my portable four-inch black and white TV set that is shaped like a loaf of bread with the tiny screen on the long end.

The only classmates I don't hate are Baby Shamu and the Sleeping Boy. Baby Shamu is a wonderful Mexican girl who is kind of large and wears only white and black. Because of this, the popular kids call her Baby Shamu after Kalina the baby killer whale at SeaWorld that the planet fell in love with.

In Washington, D.C. it's raining horribly and Baby Sh— No, fuck the popular kids. Her name is Lupe Ibarra, and Lupe is nowhere to be seen. We're on the shitty bus waiting to leave and then it's Lupe at the top of the grassy, muddy hill running toward us and she slips and then she's sliding down the hill through the mud on her back, headed a million miles an hour toward the bus.

The kids from the left side of the bus all scramble over to the right side to watch—delirious, eyes glowing, hands pressed to the cold glass, breath fogging it, happy while poor Lupe slides down the hill on her back. The chant begins: "Baby Shamu! Baby Shamu!" and I hate them and kill them with my mind. (I sink low in my seat with my face turned to the window and I cry into the arm of my hoodie.)

The Sleeping Boy has narcolepsy and we keep losing him. He falls asleep at Lincoln's giant feet and a teacher has to carry him to the bus. He falls asleep at the Vietnam Veterans Memorial next to the vases of flowers and piles of photos and notes from family members and we all stand around him as he lies there on his side, curled up like a fetus. The Sleeping Boy isn't in any of my classes, so I don't know his name. That's why he's the Sleeping Boy and not Ian or Sam or John. As we stand there, one of the popular boys (the wicked Damien Bixby) pretends to unzip his pants then pretends to piss on the Sleeping Boy. I hate Damien Bixby and I hate the Washington Trip. I don't know which I hate more.

On our final day in D.C., we lose the Sleeping Boy for the last time. No one knows where he's fallen asleep and we're due to fly out in a few hours. Two of the teachers stay behind to look for him while we take the bus to the airport. Just like I don't know the Sleeping Boy's name, I don't know what happened to him. When you're a kid no one tells you anything and then life moves on and you forget to ask. I hope he's still there. Sleeping away in some remote corner of the Smithsonian or on the lawn of the Pentagon. Sleeping away and please don't wake him. Don't wake up, Sleeping Boy. Sleep away.

I hate the Washington Trip, but then it's New York City, and in 1989 New York City is dirty and gray and ugly and loud and I *love* it. The buildings reach so high above you; everyone dressed in black and gray walking past, and those tough, worldly kids my age alone on the subway with Walkmans, and they're reading the *Times* and dressed like tiny, cool adults. We see *The Phantom of the Opera* on Broadway. At dinner before the show, my t-bone steak slides off my plate and slaps against my white turtleneck sweater, leaving a brown stain in the shape of Africa on my chest. I love the Africa stain. I love walking past couples dressed in beautiful evening attire at the theater before the show starts with my Africa-stained shirt that looks like someone took a shit on me. Because I am 14 and angry, I love looking at the fancy people and thinking, *Look at me covered in shit, FUCK you.*

We eat sausage calzones at Sbarro, and the sausage is the size of shooter marbles and I love that. We leave the shitty, cold buses behind and ride the subway, smashed into the cars with the evening crowdcrush, all of the voices and the clanging of the tracks melded into one great jumble. I love being crushed. I love the noise.

On the last day of the Washington Trip, we go to the World Trade Center's Windows on the World restaurant at the very top of the North Tower, and we're allowed to take as much food as we want from the cafeteria line. You can only go through the line once, but whatever you can fit on a tray is yours. This is like being a movie star everyone wants to give money to or a god who doesn't have to answer any phones or questions or the toughest person on Earth who can punch anyone they want to death.

I load my tray up with two beautiful cheeseburgers, three warm chocolate chip cookies so fresh they bend and fall apart when I pick them up, a peanut butter and banana sandwich, a bowl of green Jell-O with bright white whip cream, and a cobb salad I know I won't eat. But best of all? The best thing that has ever happened to me? As many snack-size bags of Nacho Cheese Doritos as I can balance on top of the rest of the food. "I love NY" says the pin I bought in the gift shop and it's true, I love NY.

I set the tray on a table by the wall of windows and take a bag of Doritos with me and stand at the glass, eating the chips. There is something magical about Nacho Cheese Doritos. They crunch perfectly and they are tangy, almost spicy, and salty all at once. Nacho Cheese Doritos are satisfying in ways that are hard to quantify. If you think about it too much, you will lose your mind.

They are perfection and questioning perfection is to scream at a wall. Why scream when you can sit back and enjoy the sublimity of whole corn, vegetable oil (corn, canola, and/or sunflower oil), corn dextrin, salt, cheddar cheese (milk, cheese cultures, salt, enzymes), whey, monosodium glutamate, buttermilk, romano cheese (part-skim cow's milk, cheese cultures, salt, enzymes), whey protein concentrate, onion powder, corn flour, natural and artificial flavor, dextrose, tomato powder, lactose, spices, artificial color (including yellow 6, yellow 5, red 40), lactic acid, citric acid, sugar, garlic powder, skim milk, red and green bell pepper powder, disodium inosinate, and disodium guanylate.

People will go to bat for Cool Ranch and I get that, but for my 14 year old money, the standard is the standard for a reason. Nacho Cheese Doritos work like all great inventions; they function in lovely, flawless, practical ways like the windmill, the Buck Knife, the rudder, and the wheel.

Standing at the window it feels as if the glass is slanted enough that you're leaning out over the city instead of standing up straight. I stuff my empty chip bag in my back pocket then press my body to the glass. It's a straight drop to beautiful nothingness—the gray streets below like strips of shoelaces with taxis and cars and buses so small you can hardly make out the details.

I close my eyes and set the side of my face against the glass and hold my ear to it and hear a deep, low breath of sound like the humming of some ancient subterranean engine.

My eyes snap back open when I feel the building move.

The building is moving.

It's swaying just slightly with the wind and with its weight, and the feeling is glorious. It's a feeling like flying, like riding on the breeze, like jumping off into nothing and falling forever.

A man in black work pants and a light blue button-up shirt who looks just like Rocky Balboa stands next to me with a mop in a yellow plastic cleaning bucket.

"Eyyy, you feel it move, donchu?" he says.

I tell him I thought I was imagining it.

"Naw, you ain't imagining nothing," he says. "This building, it's so tall it sways. It sways like this." He tips forward a little, then back. "It sways like it can't stay awake or something. Like it needs some sleep. Get some sleep, building! Take a nap!"

We both laugh and he says the part about the building taking a nap again and it's funnier the second time.

"Are we safe?" I ask.

He laughs. "I dunno. Yeah? Maybe? I been workin' here like three weeks and it freaks me out sometimes but ... ey, it's a good job. You get *this* view. You can't argue with that."

I tell him they let us take as much food as we want.

"No shit? Eyyy, nothin' wrong with that. I want *your* job. *Thas* the job you want. Tell your boss t'hire me!"

On the 11th of September, 2001, this restaurant and everything in it will be blown to pieces when American Airlines Flight 11 hits the North Tower—all of the tables, the chairs, the serving line, the cash registers, the beautiful windows, the people in the room, every single one of them gone, maybe that wonderful man with his mop and cleaning bucket, that sweet and tough funny guy.

To this day I think of it often. I think of those windows and the laughing man. I think of the blue sky and I think of the gray world below and the feeling of the glass on my cheek as the building swayed so gently.

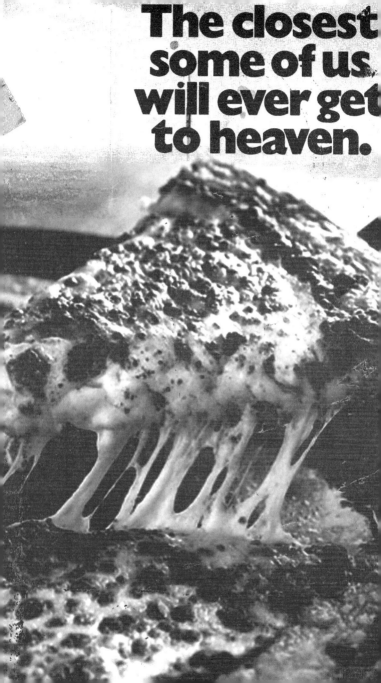

The closest
some of us
will ever get
to heaven.

PIZZA DELIVERY

****

When I know a pizza is on its way, I get very excited, and march around the room, swinging my arms side to side. I sing a pizza song to the tune of "Funiculì, Funiculà" where the lyrics are, "Pizza, pizza! Stick it in a bowl! Pizza, pizza! Weeth some guac-a-moll! Funiculì, funiculì, funiculì, funiculàhhhh! Weeth a great a-pizza make a great Italian meal! Hey!" after which the lines are repeated over and over again until the pizza arrives or my parents get mad.

I sing the pizza song during the worst days of middle school. The pizza song is triumphant over anything Pacific Beach Middle can throw at me. I sing it during 6th, 7th, and 8th grade in the lowest hole of my first depression. I sing it on nights after I've been beat up. After I've been chased home, kicked, ridiculed, embarrassed, and slandered.

I stop singing this song in high school when I am 15.

I stop singing it because high school is worse than anything I could've ever imagined.

No song sung.

Even when my parents ask, "Should we order a pizza?"

No song sung.

Even when the pizza is on its way.

No song sung.

Even when the pizza man stands in the dim light at the screen door and the dog runs to greet him, barking barking.

adaRange
Chef
BOYARDEE
CHOMPS-a-LOT
Cheese
Ravioli
80 W
150 W
450 W
780 W
1
2
3
4
5
6
7
8
9
M
C
Stop
Miele

CANNED RAVIOLI

****

Maybe you have a secret self, one that hides within your chest, is buried so deep inside there's no trace to be seen. Sometimes that's the nice you, the vulnerable you, the one who has been hurt so many times you burrow like a mouse in a grassy hillside.

The secret me walks home from school on a blustery, chilly afternoon in San Diego, the ragged heads of the palm trees lashing in the wind and the wind tearing at my clothes, the world enormous and jarring and grotesque. Because why? Because talking to people when you are friendless is terrible. Being hated is terrible. Sitting in classrooms surrounded by those who hate you is terrible. Watching their terrible cars pass by is terrible as they leave the terrible school parking lot and you are alone and you will be alone the whole walk home, and alone at home while your parents work late.

Home now.

Coming in from the cold.

Locking the door behind me.

Twice.

Two locks—the deadbolt and the lock on the handle because otherwise I feel unsafe.

Okay. Good.

An empty, quiet house, and I turn on the squat gray plastic tower heater with its red grill that turns slowly and makes a sound like someone indecisive saying, "Ummmm?"

In the kitchen I take a can of Chef Boyardee's cheese ravioli from the cupboard, open it, and dump it in a bowl. I look at Boyardee's smiling face on the can and I whisper, "Fuck you, Boyardee."

The bowl goes into the microwave for two minutes, then *ding!*

When it comes out it's steaming and too hot to eat.

I sit at the dining room table with the "Currents" section of the *Union-Tribune* in front of me and the window on the other side of the table showing the gray, stormy afternoon, and I eat and read Karla Peterson's column and burn my mouth and Jesus fucking Christ I hate Boyardee.

But the thing is, I love him too.

I secretly love Boyardee and coming in from the cold and feeling the hot food in my belly after such a stupid day.

Thank you, Boyardee, the secret me says.

Thank you for your shitty hot food.

But it's not enough.

Nothing is enough when you're 15 years old.

The greatest thing about surviving 15 is not being 15 anymore.

TRY A TRUE SPAGHETTI TREAT!

A SQUARE MEAL for THREE, 38

Here's food rich in energy and full of flavor at a price mighty easy on the pocketbook. Everybody likes spaghetti. Now it's twice as tempting as ever before. Chef Boiardi puts a bundle of fine spaghetti, a glass of genuine grated Italian cheese, and a big jar of his famous sauce all in one package for 38c. A rare, toothsome meal for three! The sauce makes the big difference. Fat mushrooms, bursting their skins, blended with fresh farm-killed beef, and the finest vine-ripened tomatoes. Give the family a treat. Order Chef Boy-ar-dee Spaghetti Dinner from your nearest independent or chain grocery store.

1 THE CHEF'S FAMOUS SAUCE
2 DELICIOUS ITALIAN CHEESE
3 HARD DURUM SPAGHETTI
ALL IN ONE PACKAGE!

CHEF BOY-AR-DEE *Instant* SPAGHETTI DINNER

BURRITOS, VARIOUS

****

When you make sense to someone it is a lovely thing. What you are doesn't tire them or make them nervous or scare them off. They see you and you make sense. Your weird shit makes sense. Your fears and delusions make sense. The things you love make sense. If you don't make sense, it's like a bitter flavor in a thing that should be sweet and it's confusing to people. They don't get you, and because they don't get you, you've got no chance of being their friend. At 16 I want nothing more than to make sense to people, but I don't make sense to anyone. Something about me is off and people my age see it and shy away. Adults like me, but that's not what a kid wants. As a kid the thing you want most is to be accepted by other kids. There are kids at school who don't make sense to most people, but they've found others who are like them and they form protective circles. I see them in the halls in leather jackets with spray paint on the back or thrift shop t-shirts or old lady cardigans. The mod girl with a stack of flyers under her arm. The Mexican boy with the mohawk who plays drums in a band. The pack of goths in fishnets and paisley and Robert Smith hair. I don't know how this works. How to talk to people. How to make sense. So I float along like a ghost and my ghost wish is for no one to see me. Mostly they don't. I come to class on time. I do the bare minimum to earn C minuses and sometimes a B. I think about dying. I get by.

After school I walk down Mission Boulevard to the goth punk store Gamma Gamma and browse the racks of posters—Siouxsie Sioux, the Smiths, Kate Bush, Iggy Pop, Bauhaus, the Sex Pistols, PiL, Joy Division, the Damned, the Sisters of Mercy. I look at pentagrams and peace symbols on silver chains and band buttons and studded leather belts and I want nothing more than that. I want to be a part of that. Or something. Anything.

I sit on the boardwalk alone every day and watch the sea and eat burritos from the Mexican restaurant by

Hamel's surf shop. Carne asada with guacamole, french fries, melted cheese, and sour cream. Chicken burritos where the folded end of the tortilla is wet with broth. Green chile and shredded beef burritos. The sea dark blue and the sky cloudless as far as you can see. The waves in tumbling lines of whitewash. A plane towing a banner reading The Big One is Back—Circus Vargas or the Velvet Touch—This Man Wants to Clean Your Clothes or If You Want a Car or Truck Go See Cal.

I sit and watch the sea and eat burritos and in this way I make sense to myself and the world makes sense too.

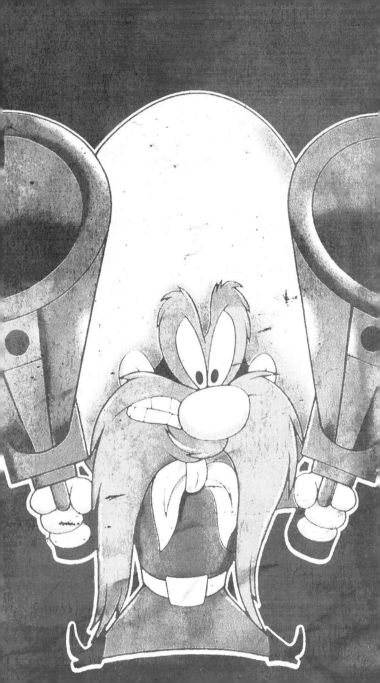

WINNER'S CHILI

****

Driving up the coast alone the week after graduation I pull off the road to stretch my legs at a scenic over-look and stare down at a valley of pine trees and distant mountains, a sunset like some pink spirit coming from the heavens to take me. It's beautiful. The endless, hazy skyline. The mellowing of the day. The sharp, clean, cit-rus scent of pine. The thought of being taken.

I sit down in the dry, prickly grass and stare at the woods and the mountains, and I feel smaller than a peb-ble in the dirt, a grain of sand on a beach with a shore as long as time.

I feel like a baseball someone has hit out of the park and is now soaring into the darkness of the sky above the parking lot and neighborhood, forgotten as the players run the bases. Someone will find that baseball in the gutter and give it to a dog and tell the dog, "Go play," and the dog will begin his work of ripping the skin off the ball. Or they'll leave it there to rot slowly with all the fallen leaves and candy wrappers and cigarette butts.

This makes me feel like you do in a dream when you're trying to hit some asshole who has come to attack you and your fists hardly connect, your spaghetti arms swing and flop and miss. When you're lucky enough to land a punch, the person you want to hurt doesn't feel a thing. It's a total lack of power. It's helplessness, frail-ty—a feeling like that of a ghost who can touch no one.

My head's whipped up in a storm. I can't get my thoughts focused on anything long enough to be a real person or to know how I am or whom I should be.

High school is over and I am blown by the wind. My world is a windblown world. My world is standing alone in the tall grass with the wind blowing, and not in a cool cinematic way that would make people love me. This is a lonely, desperate way where darkness is coming and in the woods beasts wait to hunt me.

That night I sleep in my car on the shore of a lake and at sunrise I walk up a gravel path to the cabin restaurant where fishermen eat breakfast before they put their boats in the water. It's silent on the walk and I hear nothing but the soft cry of mourning doves and the musical trilling of marsh birds as my sneakers crunch across the gravel.

The surface of the lake reflects the hills in a perfect mirror image of light green and the darkest clay-brown, an upside-down world where everything is the same except standing on its head.

I could look at that forever, stare into its depths, love it for its profound quiet, but it is a cold morning and I need to eat.

In the cabin restaurant I take a seat at a dark wooden table in the middle of a large room made entirely from the same dark wood. There are trophy fish on the walls and antlers and snowshoes and antique rifles, and the room is full of older men in ski jackets or camo coats, flannel shirts, wool hats, trucker caps, sitting in packs of three or four with steaming cups of coffee in front of them or freshly delivered meals or the remnants of breakfast. Plates streaked yellow from egg yolk. A ravaged pancake like a warzone. Some of the men are smoking at their tables because it's 1994 and in 1994 you can do that. The room smells like cigarette smoke. Not breakfast. Old cigarettes, cigarette butts, ashtrays. It's an okay smell. A grandparent smell.

As I open the menu, I hear a man at a table behind me say, "*Well*. Dig in." (He says "Well" like "Whale" and for a moment I'm confused. Where is the whale? When it dawns on me what he actually said, I feel stupid and slow and too fucked-up to exist.)

The waitress walks past carrying a plate with a stack of pancakes, and as she passes by she tells me, "Don't worry! Be right with you!"

The menu isn't complicated, but it covers a lot of bases.

The idea of having to choose something makes me want to explode.

I want everything.

I want nothing.

No, I want everything.

Especially:

Eggs Benedict $3.99, sub. biscuits for English muffins add $1

Biscuits and Gravy $3.00

Cowboy Steak and Eggs $7.50

Cheese Omelet $3.00

Denver Omelet $3.00

Spanish Omelet $4.00

Penny's Pancake Platter $3.99

Breakfast Sides $1 each: 1 egg, extra hollandaise, hash browns, 1 pancake, 3 strips bacon, 1 link sausage, 1 slice ham, 1 slice Canadian bacon, 1 English muffin, 1 buttermilk biscuit, 1 slice toast, wheat, rye, white, sour-dough

Club Sandwich $1.99

Grilled Cheese $1.99

Chicken Fried Steak $6.50

Chicken Fingers $3.50

Captain Johnny's Catch, filet of fish, scallops, shrimp $8.99

Hamburger $3.50

Cheeseburger $3.99

BBQ Burger Special, BBQ sauce, onion rings, cheddar cheese, $4.50

Patty Melt $4.50, add sauteed mushrooms $1

Reuben $4.00

Pastrami Sandwich $4.00

Chili Fries $3.50

Winner's Chili $2.50

Chicken Pot Pie $3 (Here I notice a typo in the menu. "Die" instead of "Pie." Chicken Pot Die.)

Lunch-Dinner Sides, mashed potatoes and gravy $2, cornbread $1, dinner roll .75 cents, fries $1, onion rings $1, corn on the cob .50 cents, applesauce .50 cents, house salad .75 cents, cobb salad $1, Caesar salad $1.50, fruit salad .50 cents

$1 each, coffee, tea, hot chocolate, Coke, 7-Up, Dr. Pepper, root beer, lemonade, milk, tomato juice, grapefruit juice, cranberry juice, grape juice, apple juice, orange juice

$1.99 each, slice of apple pie, cherry, peach, blueberry, strawberry rhubarb, blackberry, razzleberry, chocolate silk, banana cream

When the waitress comes, I order a cup of hot chocolate and the Winner's Chili. "Good choice," says the girl. She's wearing one of those aprons that tie at the waist and cover your pants but not your shirt. A cocktail apron. It has a row of pockets in front. From one of the pockets, she takes a small spiral-bound pad and a pen and begins writing.

"We make the chili here, my dad does," the girl says as she writes. "Nothin' from the can. He's won a buncha chili contests with it and was on the news once up in Eugene. He might go to Boston for their big one."

I ask if the chili is spicy and she says, "A little bit, but don't worry."

The girl is my age, and she has no hair or eyebrows. She's very pale with deep, creased, dark wells under her light blue eyes just like mine.

On her oversized white t-shirt is the cartoon prospector Yosemite Sam and he has both guns pointed in my direction with absurdly large barrels. His pink bottom lip frowns beneath his glorious red mustache (like two fox tails), and his eyes (which I realize at that moment look like eggs) are furious.

When the girl brings my breakfast, the chili comes in a large white bowl with a side of diced onions, a stack of saltine crackers, a square of cornbread with two pats of butter in gold foil next to it, and a small plate of grated cheddar. It smells like the sum of all good things and the negation of the world's ceaseless horseshit.

My parents think I should be a high school teacher. I'm enrolled at a junior college in Clairemont. The plan is to start in September and the idea fills me with dread. All of it. Teaching. College. There being a September.

I pick up my spoon and I eat.

THANK YOU
THANK YOU
THANK YOU
THANK YOU
THANK YOU
THANK YOU

Have a Nice Day

WARNING: TO AVOID DANGER OF SUFFOCATION, KEEP THIS PLASTIC BAG AWAY FROM BABIES AND CHILDREN. DO NOT USE THIS BAG IN CRIBS, BEDS, CARRIAGES OR PLAYPENS. THE PLASTIC BAG COULD BLOCK NOSE AND MOUTH AND PREVENT BREATHING. IN FACT, THIS PLASTIC BAG IS SO DESTRUCTIVE TO THE ENTIRE ENVIRONMENT THAT IF YOU REALLY CARE ABOUT THE FUTURE YOU COULD SERIOUSLY JUST REUSE PAPER BAGS FROM HERE ON OUT. THIS BAG IS NOT A TOY.

DON'T BE AN ACCESSORY. TO MAKE THE 100 BILLION PLASTIC BAGS THE U.S. USES EACH YEAR IT TAKES 12 MILLION BARRELS OF OIL.

CHORIZO BURRITO

****

After high school, I find friends at Mesa College, and I find friends at the restaurant jobs I work. My new friend Chente Ramirez and I live off chorizo burritos from local drive-thrus. Chente and I love them because they are spicy, dense, and hot, and that's just what you need after ruining yourself hopping from party to bar like a dumb frog and haunting the streets of Tijuana with various creatures of the night. Troubled souls like sweet tough guy softy Joey Carr, who smokes crystal like it's cigarettes, and lies about even the simplest of things.

Take a look if you will at the chorizo burrito. Eggs scrambled up with the greasy meat from all the parts of animals you don't want to know about and should never eat. The tortilla folded around it, and don't forget the tortilla is the innocent party here. A tortilla is a guardian angel in a world where angels are made up to scare you. A tortilla loves and protects everyone. It is crying about your sins as we speak. The chorizo on the other hand is a motherfucker wearing a t-shirt that reads, "Yes, he's right, I'm a motherfucker," and it will kick your ass later and you will know you have had your ass kicked and you will give it a great letter of recommendation to any job or school in America.

Friday night it's me and Chente and Joey Carr or whomever else and the glowing orange and white menu signs as big as a wall, and the fog in the streets after midnight—gentle, beautiful fog drifting up from the canyons, draping the world silently until you live within its gray shroud and everything feels hushed and secret and important.

Or it's Saturday night, ordering at the drive-thru. A carload of drunk friends just back from Tijuana. The smell of beery breath, onion sweat, Tres Flores hair grease, cigarettes, then it's laughter from the backseat and a conversation in quick, slurring, happy Spanish with a little English or English with a little Spanish. A New York Dolls tape in the deck plays low and fuzzy, David Johansen singing, "it's haaaaard/it's sooo haaard" as Chente leans across me and tells the menu wall, "*Me gustaría quatro burritos de chorizo sin huevo,*" I want four chorizo burritos without egg—without because the taste is stronger and spicier that way.

Chente Ramirez is a modern Chicano punk rocker dressed like the 1950s—greased black hair in a swooping pompadour, black sleeveless shirt, a switchblade in the pocket of his jeans, a clear and dulcet voice, and a desire to push, to live, to get better, to refine your actions, to put everything you have into all that you do. His band is the GraveTones. Yesterday I put them on a mixtape with the Misfits, the Cramps, and Ritchie Valens, and I called that mixtape "truerocknroll," one word because truerocknroll has no time for spaces. Truerocknroll has too much to do. It does not wait.

Chente looks like Lou Diamond Phillips playing Ritchie in *La Bamba* so his nickname is Ritchie, but sometimes he acts like Ritchie's wildcat brother Bob. Chente plays guitar like Ritchie's ghost is possessing him, like Chuck Berry is in his heart and Johnny Thunders is in his soul. The GraveTones scare all the white club owners because GraveTones fans are Chicano punks who love to get drunk and fight, which means no one will book them. They play houseparties. Tour on the other side of the border. Open for Mexican death metal bands and *Chilango* rock groups at Oceanside salsa clubs the bands rent out for the night.

Chorizo burritos are there if we are there and if we are there chorizo burritos are there. Stick a knife in us and tell a doctor to test the blood and the DNA will say, "Mostly chorizo."

With or without a party of friends, Chente and I drive and we talk about what we think is good, what we don't like, what we want at that very moment, nothing long-term. We are wrapped in the loose and vibrant arrogance of youth that tells you there is no future. To believe in the future is to lose momentum, to give up on the urgency and mystery of the night. There are things we want desperately to find and people we want to be and if we could put off searching until tomorrow, until next week, we might stop looking altogether. Chances are we will be disappointed. But the possibility of a life-changing night is enough to keep us in the streets. Waiting. Driving. Trying. No future. The burritos in their yellow paper wrapping drip a reddish orange clear oil. No future. They are heavy in our hands as we sit drunk to hell in the car in a San Ysidro stripmall parking lot at 3am devouring them. No future. The flour tortilla dry-grilled and chewy, the chorizo full of heat. No future.

No future.
No future.
None.
What happens tomorrow?
Nothing. There isn't one. Exactly. You got it.

TACOS AL PASTOR

****

Chente Ramirez and I are eating al pastor in Tijuana on a Monday afternoon after drinking all day at clubs like Safari, Escape, and Peanuts and Beer where it's dark as night inside and the blacklight is on and everything white glows neon green, even your teeth as the waiter grabs your head and blows a whistle then pours tequila down your throat while all the grinning white neon green college kids shout *Uno! Dos! Tres!* and on up to ten, though most quit at *cinco* because they can't remember *seis*.

Chente and I are eating al pastor under a great black sky with gray clouds like long, outstretched fingers on the walk back from the Friday *luchas* fights at the *Auditorio*. Al pastor, I call it the quivering meat wheel conception, and the man behind the counter at the stand just off *Revolución* is hacking at a rotisserie spit of dark red pork, but when you look close, if you're sober enough to notice, you will see his knife barely hits the meat, it shaves, takes a layer off like a breath. He's good. Fast. Cuts like some sort of late-night ER surgeon who is here to save your life from hunger.

After this, he chops the pile of shavings on the counter into smaller bits and sets it all with the gentlest touch in the fold of a corn tortilla followed by cilantro, diced onions, and a thin, watery avocado cream.

Hot sauce is your choice and you do it yourself if you want it—fiery red or mild green from plastic squeeze bottles. I choose the green, the tomatillo. Chente, the red.

You do that or you get the bacon-wrapped hotdogs from carts where the only option is that—a hotdog with bacon wrapped around it then fried hard. Maybe ketchup. Maybe onions. If you're lucky it's one of those terrible hotdogs with a vein of cheese in the center. A hotdog injected with Cheez Whiz.

Avenida Revolución. Revolution Avenue. "We were hangin' out down on Revolution," we say when we refer to it.

The street smells like cigars, muffler exhaust, leather, frying onions, and sewage. If it were a cologne, we would wear it. Were it a drink, we would take shots.

Chente and I are sitting on the curb. It's a moonless Sunday night and we're singing two different New York Dolls songs at once and stuffing our faces, drunk out of our minds, ecstatic with the moment. Al pastor is sweet and salty and hot, and when it hits your stomach your stomach is quiet, balanced, thankful that you've made such a smart choice.

Chente and I are walking back to the border at dawn on a Tuesday from a bad night at the cowboy bar on *Calle Miguel Hidalgo* with an al pastor taco in each hand, eating slowly, mostly talking—talking about what the hell's wrong with people and why is everyone such a colossal tower of shit or how we can't feel at home in this world anymore, like the words of the old folk song.

> "This world is not my home
> I'm just a-passin' through
> My treasures are laid up
> Somewhere beyond the blue
> The angels beckon me from Heaven's open door
> And I can't feel at home
> In this world anymore"

O' beyond the blue. Chente and I, tacos in hand, eating, talking, say nothing about heaven because we've stopped believing long ago that there is anything beyond death.

You die.

You are gone.

We say things like that when we talk about death. (Him, with certainty. Me, not so certain.) We go to Tijuana and we drink beer and tequila and we talk to people and sometimes we get in fights. We eat tacos from the many al pastor carts and we renounce this world that is not our home. This world? It's not mine. Fuck it. I'm passing through. Like another old folk song:

"Passing through
Passing through
Sometimes happy
Sometimes blue
Glad that I ran into you
Tell the people
That I'm only passing through"

AUNT SOREL'S LASAGNA

****

Joey Carr says he's been driving down to the beach in the morning because it feels weird to live on the coast and never go there. He tells me he's been staying up all night shooting speed then taking some kind of breakfast with him on the passenger seat of his truck and driving down to Sunset Cliffs where he'll sit on the rocks and eat and watch the sea and the tide pools as he's coming down. Today's meal was leftover lasagna from a rare dinner at his aunt and uncle's place in Pacific Beach. Aunt Sorel's lasagna. Sorel is a dreadful word. It sounds like a euphemism for shitting your pants. "He soreled his pants." "She got really drunk at the party and soreled her jeans in her sleep." Joey's uncle's name is Jake and that's okay. You can't fuck up a name like Jake. Uncle Jake is a terrible person, but at least his name isn't gross.

Joey tells me he parked in the dirt lot at Point Loma Nazarene next to a van with a bunch of surfers changing out of their wetsuits and carried the glass casserole dish with its black plastic spatula wedged under the side of the last half of the lasagna and walked along the weedy, scrub brush trails until he found a nice, secluded spot to eat. He thought about Garfield as he walked. How much Garfield hates Mondays. How he tries to send his enemies to Abu Dhabi. How Garfield loves lasagna. As a kid, Joey had always looked up to Garfield. Wished he could be more like him. Be orange, be a cat, fat too, a fat cat who is maybe violently insane but always good for a laugh. Garfield the hilarious, dangerous psychopath.

Joey says he sat on the cliffside and ate with the spatula. Ate layers of cold pasta and ricotta, tomato sauce and Italian sausage, picked out the black olives and tossed them to the ants, ate and watched the ants eat and watched the gray, smooth expanse of the sea, the waves rolling in, slow but large as mountains, and out near the kelp beds the groups of surfers waiting to catch one.

Joey says his aunt Sorel is the worst cook in the world, but her lasagna is a fine thing. Joey doesn't say "fine thing." He says, "Really good," but I am translating it as fine thing because I see how much he means it. The thing about Joey Carr is he means it. He wants to be tough and he wants to be sarcastic, but he's bad at both. At the core of Joey is an earnest child trying to speak directly in the center of all the noise of life. Often you don't see or hear that child, but if you listen and look close he's there, waiting patiently, unsmiling, choleric, dark-eyed, cold as if forever seeking shelter from an autumn storm. It's a fading glimmer in him like the dying light of a lantern, but that is the true and secret Joey.

Joey says he's gotta split. He's gotta go home and sleep this off. He knows he's going to fall hard this time. Maybe this is it, he says. Maybe this is the last time. When he says that I think, If Joey Carr dies, I'll just *die*.

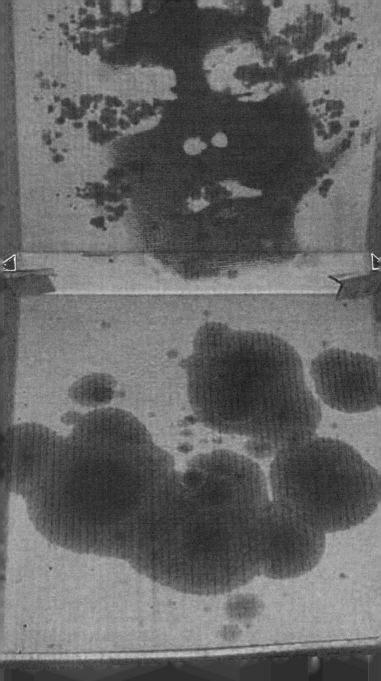

NEW YORK PIZZA

****

In the 1982 film *Conan the Barbarian*, a Mongol war-lord asks Conan what is best in life and Conan answers, "Crush your enemies, see them driven before you, and hear the lamentation of their women." If that warlord were to ask Chente and Joey and me the same question, we would answer, "1970s New York rock 'n' roll." Chente is the Mexican Johnny Thunders. Tough, earnest Joey wants to be Richard Hell who was famous for wearing a torn shirt with "Please Kill Me" written across the front and playing songs that were like a vampire Jerry Lee Lewis. I pretend I'm Patti Smith and go off by myself and stare at the sea or kick a wall of glass windows in because Jesus died for somebody's sins but not mine. We listen to the Velvets on cassette in Joey's truck as we drive three to a cab down the 5 to Tijuana and Joey rolls his window down and smokes and Chente tells him he's gross for smoking and Joey laughs and flicks his cigarette into the night (the butt end skipping through the darkness, sparks bouncing up from it). We carry switchblades and Joey's got brass knuckles he bought in TJ. We drive, brakes smearing red and the lights of the freeway at night blurring, and maybe we're half-drunk or Joey's high from wrapping little bits of crystal in Wonder Bread and eating it on the sly so Chente doesn't see, and we listen to Lou Reed singing,

> "If I could make the world as pure
> And strange as what I see
> I'd put you in the mirror
> I put in front of me
> I put in front of me
> Linger on
> Your pale blue eyes"

—and we consider the authority in his words and say nothing during the quiet, gentle, aching guitar solo over the barest hit of a tambourine because maybe if you're respectful enough, quiet enough, open enough to the possibilities, you can live inside a song.

Richard Hell sings, "But I rip up my shirt/watch the mirror it flirt," and we're right there with him in the rock 'n' roll club.

Johnny Thunders sings about how you can't put your arms around a memory, and we think we know just what he means. (We don't. Not yet. But we will.)

Joey is Chente's best friend and he's further in than me. I like to hide indoors because my anxiety eats me these days like a pile of maggots on a dead seagull. I am a flightless pile of bones and feathers on the sand. I am a piece of shit covered in a pile of shit covered in a mountain of it covered in a light, drifting snowdrift of shit on such a winter's day.

Drunk Joey shouts, "I want New York pizza!" one night as we drive around City Heights looking for a party we don't have the address for, and we know he wants New York pizza because he's a romantic and because he's in love with the Italy in his blood. He wants to live some *Blank Generation, White Light/White Heat* life none of us will ever know because that time has passed. Joey Carr is a poser and I'm a poser too. Chente's not a poser because he lives it. But me and Joey? Ugh, we're the worst people in the world. We're babies, dumb-asses, fakes, wannabes, dead birds, shit upon shit upon shit upon shit.

"I want New York pizza!" drunk-shouted while driving to a party means I want a life I am not living. We're not cool, tough New York kids in leather jackets and black sunglasses. We are restless Californians. Chente from the wastelands of the Imperial Valley with its car mechanics, cholos, desert stripmalls, crabgrass lawns, and rabbits raised in backyards for food. Joey and I are P.B. boys, beach kids, Pacific Beach nobodies. We eat Mexican food, Americanized spaghetti shop Italian, and seafood. That is the cuisine of our hometown, but New York pizza is Tom Verlaine, Marty Rev, and Alan Vega. It's living on a Chinese Rock, the plaster's falling off the wall, your girlfriend crying in the shower stall. New York pizza means the Dolls posing in front of the Gem Spa.

It means Warhol, Candy Darling, Edie Sedgwick, Jayne County singing "Stuck on You." It's Robert Quine's slashing guitar notes. It's Nico, the Ramones, Harry Smith, the Chelsea Hotel, Robert Mapplethorpe, El Quijote, Max's Kansas City, CBGB, and the Mercer Arts. We know about that from books like *Please Kill Me* and *From the Velvets to the Voidoids*. What we really know is Belmont Park with the clacking rollercoaster and red balloons and waffle cones. We know the Livewire, the Lamplighter, the Casbah, the yellow-lit O.B. pier at night with hustlers waiting for johns and shitty white hippies playing "Redemption Song" on acoustic guitar and getting the words wrong. We know Pacific Eyes and T's, Mossy Nissan moves youuuu, Fashion Valley, the Crowbar, Balboa Park, Vinyl Communications, Antioch Arrow, People's, Eyton Shalom, Tourettes Lautrec, the Claw and the Crypt, Tredair UK in Hillcrest, Deadbolt, KUSI, 91X, Tony McCune of McCune Chrysler-Plymouth and his dog called "Honest," Swindle's bad hair on the Jones Soda bottle, King Stahlman's Bail Bonds, the P.B. Block Party, Crash Worship, the Sports Arena Tower, SOMA, the Unarius Academy of Science, "Shotgun Tom" Kelly, Jeff and Jer, John Reis, Flashbacks, and Kobey's Swap Meet. We know the Santee drive-in full of rednecks with lift-kit trucks and a pistol under the seat. We know the Ken Club and a line to do coke in the bathroom and everyone's got that San Diego mod Spock pixie hairdo including me and they're talking a mile a minute and it's so dumb I want to find someone with a stick to hit me so I burst like a piñata and spill all my candy out. We know the best places to have sex in a car where the cops won't bother you. We know the Hillcrest Landmark and many people who have worked there as projectionists. We know Tecolote Canyon, Green Valley Falls, Off the Record, Robb Field, Gelato Vero, and famous Ken "the Flash" Hellingson who rollerskates the boardwalk wearing nothing but a thong and holiday appropriate head gear—a Santa Claus hat and beard on Christmas or his body painted red, white, and blue for the 4th, an Uncle Sam hat on his head, and a blazing sparkler tucked into the strap of his g-string. We know

"Dead" Alan whom you will see at bars and shows carrying his wizard's staff with fake heads tied to it. We know Lou's, the Shake Rag, Faque Burger, the 163, the 8, the 5, the 805, and the 15. We know the Golden Dragon. We know Mandarin Dynasty and how if you're a punk or any sort of weirdo and you show up with a big group you will get a random assortment of free sodas as some sort of bohemian solidarity hookup. We don't care about any of that because we want a thing we cannot have.

Chente has plans to move to New York City and none of our friends believe he'll do it. They think he's just a dead-end Chicano boy from El Centro, but I know him well enough that I have no doubt he'll do it and be good at it and we won't see him again unless we visit. Anyone who underestimates Chente Ramirez is in for a shock.

Joey shouts, "I want New York pizza!" but we never get New York pizza. We eat sopes and we eat shredded beef rolled tacos and endless burritos but New York pizza? I remember machaca, carnitas, chicken burritos from Adalberto's down on Market and 25th with all the finest drug dealers, tostadas at El Zarape on Park, fish tacos at Rubio's in P.B., lobster bisque in Ocean Beach when we had the money, shrimp and chips with a sourdough roll at Point Loma Seafoods, but New York pizza? No. When we do get pizza it's just pizza. Domino's. Shakey's. Godfather's. Nothing special.

Joey picks fights with bigger guys at bars and nine times out of ten he's beat to hell. I sit alone at parties and stare out at the world from inside my shell and I feel ugly. I think, Fuck everything, fuck this whole fucking place. I reconsider my choices. I'd rather hide in a dark cave like the fishermen pray in. I spend my spare time at the used bookstore, and when I bring books to the counter, the old, scraggly, hippy troll sitting in his chair says snide shit about my choices. I want to be a kind, gentle, moral person, but I kill him with my thoughts. I tear his shitty head off and I rip his crooked backbone out and cook it over a fire to feed a bunch of hungry animals, but really I do nothing. I'm a quiet kid. I'm nice. I'm fragile. I don't want violence or wild nights. I want to read books in safe, warm places and listen to records and see my friends when I want (but only when I want). I want to set my limits with friendship.

"Real healthy," you say, your voice downright gory with sarcasm.

You're right, though. You're right.

THEME (Main) BUILDING
Los Angeles Airport

99-CENT BREAKFAST

****

Often when someone you love moves away, you never see them again. You make plans to visit their new place, and they make plans to visit you, and you write letters or emails. But those letters, those emails become fewer and fewer with greater spaces in between until they stop entirely. The plans you made don't pan out because they've got a new life, and you've got your old one, and the responsibilities of maintaining both get in the way. Goodbyes hurt so much I'd rather not do them at all. Just slip out the back way and be gone. Cut and run from the party without sayin' a thing. Spare yourself the pain of thinking, "Wait, maybe I'll never *see* this person again." Because you're right. Mostly, you won't. Life is very short, and it marches forward without lull or cease until you reach the final Stop sign. Then, of course, it's too late for goodbyes or hellos or letters or visits. Friends who leave are like a bookcase of books you've read. You've collected all these lovely things to read and you've read them, but most you will never pick up again. You might intend to, but the years pass by, the dust gathers, and the shadows fall.

When Chente moves to New York City I go along to help him get settled because it's easier than a hard and fast goodbye, a goodbye at the airport or at a party or a bar. On a clear, cool, sunny morning, Chente and I catch a commuter flight from San Diego to LAX, and with six hours to kill we go to the airport's sci-fi-themed restaurant. I carry Chente's old, stained, hollow body Epiphone and he carries the yellow-tan electric Gibson he played in the GraveTones. We have backpacks, but the rest he's shipped out ahead of him.

Chente and I take the elevator to the restaurant and grab a seat at the circular bar with its glittery silver counter, setting the guitars on the floor and holding their necks with our knees.

The building the restaurant is in is a beautiful, weird Mid-century Modern structure meant to look like a flying saucer, the saucer section elevated by a series of dramatic crossed arches that hold it 15 feet above the ground. In the bar you have a lovely, panoramic, 360-degree view of Los Angeles.

There is something particularly LA about the restaurant—the view out the windows of blue sky and the sun and gleaming concrete as white as snow and the palm trees and planes and tarmac; the 1960s architecture with its clean, minimalist lines and its optimistic interpretation of humanity's interaction with the future and outer space. It's a thing born of hope, belief in progressive innovation, and fraternal spirit. Of course, the future of the 1950s and '60s didn't happen. Here we are at the turn of the century and it sucks. No flying cars. No *Jetsons* sky mansions or jokey robot maids clonking about. In 1999 people are bored with space. Bored with astronauts and rockets. Bored with hoping. The place is a testament to what could have been, and what never came.

Chente orders a can of Tecate with a lime slice, and I ask for a Sierra Nevada even though I hate it, and we sit on our barstools and take in the scene.

On the big glass domed walls of the spaceship are neon green decals of stars, comets, and planets, and more of the same drifting across the dark ceiling by way of a hidden projector. The bartender, a tall blonde kid our age in black pants and a stiff white shirt sets up a drink for an older guy sitting next to Chente. It's a gin and tonic, and when he sprays the tonic water into the glass, the gun makes a canned laser sound.

The older guy takes a sip then lifts his glass in salute and the bartender says, "Y'got it, Cap."

"This place is like a shitty *Star Trek*," says Chente confidentially.

"It's cheesy, but I like it."

"What if we *lived* here?" he says.

"I'd do that."

"Imagine if this was your *living room*."

Halfway through our third beer a gray-haired woman in beige capri pants and a tight pink t-shirt shuffles up to us. Her husband, bald and potbellied with sandals, extra-long jean shorts, and a hooded red sweatshirt with a Confederate flag on the front, follows close behind, hands tucked in the front pocket of his hoodie.

The woman clears her throat dramatically to get my attention then says, "I just *knew* it was you."

Surprised, I ask her, "Who? What's me?"

Chente turns to face her, happy and confused.

The woman says, "Jimmy dihn't want me to say nothin' but—"

"Nnnope," grunts Confederate Flag Jimmy standing off to the side.

"—but oh my gawd Train is me and my daughter Linda's all-time my favorite band."

"*Train*? Wait, *what*?" I say.

"I just hadda say somethin' to you. Jimmy tried to talk me out of it."

"Yup," says Jimmy, staring off behind us at the windows. "Ah did."

Chente smiles at her and says, "You want his autograph?"

I start to tell her I'm not in the band Train, but Chente cuts me off, saying, "*Yes*, he is. He's the singer from Train and he would *love* to give you his autograph. He does it all the time. I'm his manager. I'm always telling him, 'Train, *buddy*, you needa sign more autographs. People are so *happy* when you sign autographs.' Where you all from?" he says mimicking the woman's accent just enough that she doesn't notice.

I hold my hands out in front of me. "No. Chen—"

"Don't be shy, Train," he tells me.

"We're from Jacksonville, Flarida," says the woman and Jimmy grunts something that's maybe him agreeing, maybe a growl of displeasure.

"*Give* 'em an autograph, Train," Chente says.

"Ohhh, if you would," the woman says. She digs in her purse for a pen then tugs the cocktail napkin from under my beer, spilling some of it on the silver counter. "It would mean *so* much to me."

"Hey, do you want him to sing 'Meet Virginia' because he *will*," says Chente. "Train loves singing that song. He was just singing it a minute ago. You missed it. He sings it like 12 times a day. Sing it, Train."

I feel nauseous. I try to explain how this is a case of mistaken identity and that I can't give her an autograph because I'm— but she interrupts, saying, "Oh, you doan have to if you're embarrassed."

"Yeah. I'm sorry. I just can't—"

But she's not listening to me. She says, "If you would sign it to Donna it would be so special." Now she's smiling again. Grinning like I'm about to hand her a bunch of money. "Donna with an O and two Ns."

I hate everything. I hate Chente. I hate Train. I hate LA. I hate Florida. I hate Donna and I hate Jimmy.

"Donna Fitzpatrick. That's with a Z. It's F I T Z Patrick like the Irish name. Donna Fitzpatrick."

Jimmy nods then grunts, "Arrsh," which is maybe "Irish."

I sign the cocktail napkin and hand it back to Donna Fitzpatrick.

"Oh, you're jus—" and then she's crying and waving a hand in front of her face.

Chente sings, "Meeeet Virginia," then says, "C'mon, everybody together," and continues to sing, "Meet Virginia/I can't wait to/meet Virginia."

As Chente and Donna sing together I get up without saying anything and walk to the restroom.

When I get back Donna Fitzpatrick and Jimmy the Confederate Flag are gone and Chente's ordered us another round.

"Hey, Train. What did you write on the napkin?" he asks.

I sit down on my barstool. "First, fuck you. Second, I wrote your name. I don't know the fucking Train singer guy's name, and for the record I look nothing like him."

"I only know him from the radio at work," he says. "Pretty funny, though. That fuckin' lady. Oh hi, hello, uh, hi, I'm Donna with two Ns and here's my shithead baby man husband. I just *love* your music."

"That band is garbage, Chente. I can't believe you told—"

"*Mijito, a la verga,* drink your beer. Don't be such a fuckin' *rockstar*. Oh, *sabes qué,* I ordered us some shots of tequila."

I wake up sitting in a hard plastic seat at our terminal, Chente next to me, sleeping, hunched forward, head in his hands.

Our backpacks are gone, but we've held onto the guitars.

I shake Chente's shoulder and he sits up straight and looks around, red-eyed. "What. Shit. Ugh, *carnali-to,* how did we *get* here? Is it *nighttime*?"

I tell him that I just woke up a second ago and like magic we're at the gate.

"My last memory's of being ... being in the *Star Trek* bar," he says. "Some white guy ordered a head of iceberg lettuce and they gave it to him on a plate with a fork and not even ... *motherfucker didn't even get dressing.*"

I pat the pockets of my jeans and hoodie for my wallet and find it with a rushing sense of relief.

I tell Chente, "I remember the second shot of tequila then that's it."

"Homie, where are the *backpacks*?"

"I think we lost them."

Chente sits back in his seat and puts his fingers to his temples and says, "Fuck," very quietly. Like the quietest you could ever say fuck and have it still be fuck.

On the plane we order the chicken cheddar casserole and two beers which becomes four, each with a mini bottle of Cuervo Gold.

The food arrives on a thin black plastic tray, and it looks like yellow baby shit.

I push my dinner away from me. "Nope. This is baby shit."

Chente peels the plastic off his and laughs. "I'm not eating *anything* a baby shits out."

"Ugh, I can't remember the last time we ate."

"Homie, this baby shit is ... naw, no way," he sets the plastic wrap back on it, pushing it to the far end of his table. "It looks like *mucus*. They must have a bunch of babies back there shitting mucus onto each tray."

"Or one giant baby," I offer.

"One giant baby shitting and shitting and shitting," Chente says happily.

I decide to sleep.

When I wake up the plane is dark.

Chente has his head against the window, the guitar between his knees, the window black with the tiny pin-prick lights of a city below us.

The plane rocks with a gentle hit of turbulence and the seatbelt light comes on.

Just then I realize I need to throw up.

I need to throw up *right now*.

It's coming.

Rising up fast like oil about to burst from the ground.

I click my seatbelt off and stagger down the aisles, holding the head rests for support.

A few rows later I find myself beginning to fall.

Then nothing.

When I wake up, a stewardess is squatting in front of me, patting my shoulder.

"Sir, sir. SIR. You need to get up and go back to your seat. We're landing."

My cheek pressed to the carpeted floor, I see the puddle of my vomit under the chair nearest me. The man in the chair sleeps on, unaware, mouth open like a baby bird.

In Bed-Stuy, Chente unpacks the boxes of books and vinyl records he's shipped to his beautiful, violet-eyed girlfriend Chavela who sits on the bed of the studio apartment, legs crossed at the ankles, smiling, deeply in love, excited he's here, that it's finally happening and now she can show him around, take him to all the places she's found since moving here to start school, and that is what we do. Long, drowsy afternoons riding the subway. Steamy gray streets in Chinatown with the intoxicating smell of food and dumpster garbage. Rundown, graffiti-splattered bars in Chelsea where poor Chavela sits bored though patient while Chente and I make fools of ourselves all night.

Sometimes she pulls a book out of her bag and reads. Reading Proust in a bar while her boyfriend and his idiot friend drink and act dumb. Reading critical theory while Chente stands laughing in front of the dartboard holding his beer pint up to protect his face as I throw darts at him.

We buy bootleg New York Dolls t-shirts at punk boutiques and pose for photos trying to look like tough 1970s bad-asses in front of the Gem Spa and the boarded-up space that was once the Mercer Arts Center.

In Williamsburg, we leave a bodega one night with bags of groceries for a pasta dinner, and I run right into the actor Willem Dafoe. We hit chests and stagger backward, catching ourselves just shy of falling.

I apologize profusely, staring at his gaunt, lined Willem Dafoe face, thinking, *Oh shit, you were in fucking Platoon.*

"It's awright," he says, smiling, gap-toothed, his voice gravelly, soft, good natured. "*Doan* even *warry* about it."

"Sorry, shit, sorry."

"Y'ave yourself a good evening, awright?"

We haunt the streets of Brooklyn in search of pizza because Chente vows that we must be better than that LA prick with his *Star Trek* head of lettuce no dressing and all the people slurping down baby shit on the plane.

We order Joey Carr's dream New York pizza in every shoebox Italian restaurant where the windows are steamed-up against the chill outside and the yellow taxis blur past and slices are 99 cents, thin as paper, and wide as a pyramid. Chavela, Chente, and I eat New York pizza twice a day for what feels like weeks. The soft, chewy crust with a little red sauce, a thin layer of hot, stretchy mozzarella, and sliced mushrooms that crisp up and begin to curl in the heat of the oven.

Sometimes we get sausage if they're out of plain

cheese or mushroom, but Chente says he's thinking of quitting meat so it's cheese and mushroom whenever we can get them, the slices so big and so thin you have to fold them in half down the middle and so hot you burn your mouth, but how could you *wait*?

Soon it's time for Chente to look for work, and Chavela's classes are starting up, so I go out each day alone, roaming the streets of Brooklyn with my Walkman, a book and my pocket notepad rubber-banded together, and the solitary cassette tape I'd carried with me on the plane in my hoodie pocket.

I listen to side A and walk under the swooping BQE, the wind in my face.

The mixtape is a collection of all my new favorite bands.

Side A is a few songs each from Pedro the Lion, Bright Eyes, Kind of Like Spitting, the Dismemberment Plan, Sunday's Best, the Black Heart Procession, Death Cab for Cutie, Jets to Brazil, Modest Mouse, Pinback, and At the Drive-In. On its white sticker paper label I've written "indie rock."

On the label of side B I've written "punk." Side B is a mix of Cattle Decapitation, Clikatat Ikatowi, the Beautiful Mutants, Moss Icon, X, Swing Kids, Joy Division, the VSS, the Germs, the Locust, Men's Recovery Project, and Le Shok.

I stand with my Walkman on in the immensity of Manhattan, the spider web of industry, the buildings reaching up to dizzying heights, the Twin Towers like two black tongue depressors flat against the pale blue skyline.

The music in my ears from side B is like a hurricane, a parking lot fistfight, an earthquake with blast beats and synthesizers.

Side A is a reassuring letter sent from far away, a place to find friends. It's poetry and quiet turmoil and life.

A cold spell settles in and now when you go outside you see your breath in front of you like you're smoking. On my last day in town, I wake up earlier than Chente and Chavela and I walk to a corner breakfast place called Bedford Eats.

I pull open the door, and as the bell dings, everyone turns to look at the one white kid in the place before going back to their plates.

"What's up, white folks?" says the big man behind the counter.

"I saw a sign for 99-cent breakfast?"

"You askin' me if you seen a *sign*?"

"No, I'm—"

"Dude, I'm just playin' witchu. You want bacon or sausage with that, little homie?"

"Can I just ... uh, how 'bout just, like, extra hash-browns?"

"You got it, baby. My wife vegetarian and I ain't got a problem with that. She's from Jamaica. All her people eat like that. I eat meat but she like, Boy you *gross*. In fact, I'm gonna give you extra eggs and toast. That sound a'ight?"

"That sounds amazing. Thanks."

"Niner, no meat, X eggs, X hash-b's, X toe," he shouts toward the kitchen. "Oh, hold up, what kinda toast you want?"

"Sourdough?"

"You got it, baby. Be, like, um, ten minutes."

I sit at a table by the door and wait. The diner smells like all of American breakfast rolled into one—fresh coffee, potatoes frying in onions and grease, toasting bread, bacon, pancakes, sausage. It's a smell like the home you've always wanted, the safe and lovely place where you eat what makes you feel secure and taken care of and loved. I pull the Patti Smith book I got at St Mark's out of my front hoodie pocket and I read:

"I was the wing
in heaven blue
yet to trod
in heavy shoes
of mortal worth
bound to earth

bound to earth"

A few pages later a bell in the open space between the dining room and the kitchen dings three times and the man behind the counter says, "Yo, white folks! We got some food ready for you if you ain't too busy reading! Hahaha. Come getcha breakfast, lil' bro!"

I stuff the book in my hoodie pocket and walk to the counter.

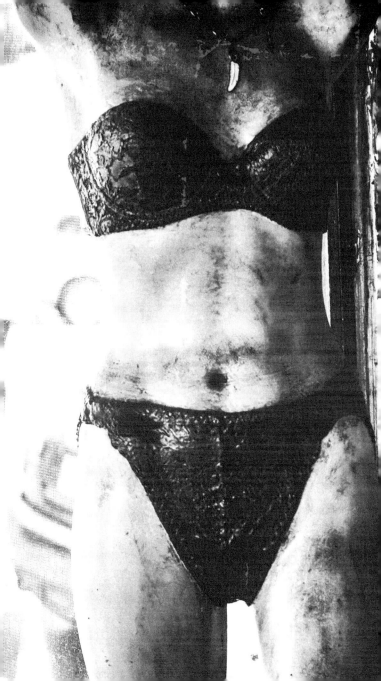

TOM'S DEEP PLATE

****

People change for countless reasons. Sometimes that change comes surging direct and pure. Immanuel Kant defined a moral imperative as something so deeply felt that it drives you to take action. You change because that change is fundamental to your principles, to your code of ethics. You are pushed by your beliefs and by your conscience. You are morally compelled by your understanding of what keeps the world running as it should and how one should be a steward of that. We also change because of fear. We change because of damage done to us. We change to survive. Then sometimes we change for no other reason than the fact that those around us are changing. We go along with the herd. This can be bad, but it can also be a kind of natural, spontaneous evolution. Not everything we do is pushed by morals, necessity, or desire.

I quit eating meat after Chente moved to New York. I quit because Chente said he was going to and because most of my new friends had done the same, and I thought nothing of it, and ate what they ate as you do when you are young and obsessed with your friends and want to live inside their lives and know the world as they know it.

New friend #1 Tyler Monahan was rail-thin and had blonde hair halfway between David Bowie and Kurt Cobain and was brilliant in a way that felt utterly foreign to me. Math smart, science smart. Tyler was both vampiric and elfin. He was also a kid. Silly. Fun. Refused to take things too seriously like I did.

I first wanted to become Tyler's friend because of his good manners. Working together in the dining room of a retirement center along with Joey Carr before he quit, I saw Tyler ask for things with a "Please" and an earnest, happy "Thank you!" and often a "Ma'am" or a "Sir," and I watched him inquire after the residents' families and their health as the rest of us drank 40s in the back office, talked atrocious shit without cease, hooked up with each other, stole whatever we could from the kitchen, and watched TV in the breakroom during our shifts.

The dining room staff at the retirement home was a monstrosity of trouble and vice. Lil' Cassidy selling acid to the cooks and maintenance guys. Sex-crazed teenagers Petra Cooper and Suzy Dillard giving head in the broom closet. Doomed Ronny Lucas staying up for a week on speed before disappearing forever down in Rosarito, showing up years later as a lower jawbone, a sun-scorched red canvas wallet, and three ribs in the desert outside Mexicali. Joey Carr coming to work candyflipping on acid and ecstasy and talking to the residents about the beautiful green eyes he had jerking back and forth underneath the skin of his chest or getting drunk with the Nigerian dishwashers and climbing into the A-C vent to sleep.

Tyler by contrast was sweet and quiet, though gently sarcastic when he cared to be. Mostly he was earnest and sincere, and I loved him for it. Maggie Harker I met through Tyler. Maggie, though wild like Chente and Joey Carr, was also very polite. She and Tyler were on again off again, and had been since they were very young, and soon Maggie and Joey Carr would get together. Everyone wanted to get laid as often as possible and with as many different partners, and most of us were terribly inexperienced, some stilted by religious upbringings (and now rebelling against that). The sum of this was a minefield, a shooting range, and a fireworks factory all in one.

The people I knew, the people I loved, were interconnected like a pile of kittens sleeping in a basket by the window or a swarm of snakes massing on the floor of a tomb. Relationships were a game of musical chairs or a crashing plane. Spontaneous, drunken threesomes. Make-out parties. Boyfriends mad at girlfriends because the girlfriends had secret girlfriends of their own. Boyfriends getting boyfriends and breaking up with girlfriends. Virginities lost dramatically and documented with Polaroids or LiveJournal erotica. Hearts broken like plates dropped on the floor, and friendships destroyed—though temporarily. This was a time when everything fixed itself like a patch of grass torn-up by car tires grown back after a few rains. The way we were was something like this: *hey*, no hard feelings.

When everyone is hurting everyone all at once and no one has any hard feelings about it, you wind up in the rare position of finding yourself an adult with nothing but good relations and positive associations regarding old friends. That protective veil over us is a thing I have seen only once, and wanted often, and I have not known better and kinder people than the ones I hurt with all the energetic, arrogant stupidity of youth.

No matter how bad things were, I would get a call or an email from the person who should hate me most, and we'd meet at Pokez in Downtown and eat together and reaffirm our friendship without saying a single word about it.

Like you do when you are hoping to avoid a subject, we would talk about things disconnected from the disaster of our connected love lives. We would talk about Saddle Creek and Gravity Records bands, and we would talk about people's hairstyles, and so and so who worked at the Catwalk and now sold heroin down in Chula Vista, and we would talk about food.

At Pokez I lived off the Tom's Deep Plate—a large, hot platter with a pile of soft orange Mexican rice, refried beans, guacamole, sour cream, salsa fresca, and a stack of flour tortillas. I ate it like Chente showed me when we first started hanging out—you tear palm-size shreds off the tortillas then use them to pinch up bits of food in neat little pockets.

Everything about the Tom's Deep Plate was the best around—the beans, peppery and smashed to a thick, creamy, pan-fried clump; the rice with peas, corn, and little cut up bits of green beans; the guacamole, fresh with just enough cilantro, salt, and lime; the salsa, almost too hot but fine, and a little smoky; the tortillas dry-grilled, dusty with flour, chewy.

Flour tortillas have always been one of my favorite parts of a meal. Wheat is good no matter what cuisine you're eating. Pasta in all its forms. Japanese noodles like ramen, soba, and udon. A good sourdough round torn to pieces and eaten with a little butter, salt, and a squeeze of lemon. Pizza crust. Breadsticks dipped in ranch or marinara. Bagels with cream cheese or an egg and cheddar. Donuts. Funnel cake. Pie crust. Black Forest cake. But tortillas? The queen of them all. Pokez' tortillas were soft and delicate but firm, cooked just enough to burn brown spots here and there.

It is a lovely thing to come from a border town in the western United States. The more taco shops your neighborhood has, the finer your life will be. To have regular access to a place like Pokez in Downtown San Diego is to be given one of the sweetest, most substantial gifts of all—a home, a cave to hide out in, a den to meet partners-in-crime, and a menu that could shove a stake into the heart of all the soulless, grim, sterile, corporate restaurants of America.

Coming from a restaurant family I knew this was what you wanted most—a small place with low overhead, a good menu but a clean and simple one, and a devoted fanbase that considered your restaurant the highest seat of society—a place to be seen, a place you wanted people to know was your regular spot, your hang-out at any time night or day.

Pokez had skate decks nailed to the walls like priceless works of art and photos of legendary hardcore bands Spanakorzo, Run for Your Fucking Life, and Guyver-One tacked up by the register. Its front door was covered layers-thick in stickers—skate company stickers, graffiti artist stickers, Holiday Matinee stickers, Slowdance Records stickers, Ché Café stickers, *Muddle* stickers, *Geek America* stickers, Shepard Fairey stickers, Insound stickers, Tiger Style stickers, Locust stickers, 91X stickers, Acamonchi stickers, Drive Like Jehu stickers. Sometimes a DJ spun mellow, contemplative, instrumental hiphop, dub, or rare grooves while you ate. Sometimes, on late afternoons, it was quiet and dark, and the sunlight from outside shone bright through the glass, and you felt an otherworldly sense of security.

Like once inside these walls no bastard can touch you. Once through this door you stand immortal. Pokez was a place big-name touring bands would stop at and you'd eat a few feet away from someone you'd seen on MTV that week, but no one bothered them because at Pokez you didn't lose your cool or get up in anyone's business. There was an unspoken rule: you eat here, you keep yourself together and don't be a fuckin' idiot. Be chill, be cool, enjoy your food, or go somewhere else. If the waiters didn't like you, you knew it. They wouldn't hold back. If they were rude to you, you deserved it.

Though the tofu fajitas and Joey's Special were not to be trifled with, I rarely if ever deviated from the Tom's Deep Plate for many months. Still drunk after house shows in Hillcrest or North Park with a Tom's Deep Plate, off work and hiding out from people in our social group who were angry with me and a Tom's Deep Plate. Alone with a copy of *Hit it or Quit It* and a Tom's Deep Plate. A party of friends and a Tom's Deep Plate.

My memories of the time taste like the Tom's Deep Plate, and they smell like it, and I can still feel the heat of the big white Pokez plate, testing it with a finger after the server sets it down, saying, "Yo, don't touch the plates. They're fuckin' *hot*, bro."

CHILE RELLENO BURRITO

****

I love the heavy, twice-folded cheese quesadillas from La Posta in Hillcrest with a side of sour cream and a can of Coke and I hate myself.

I love a beans, rice, and guacamole burrito and a small paper plate of hot carrots at Saguaro's and I hate myself.

I love a dish of refried beans with melted cheese on top and a side of corn tortillas at Sombrero in South Park and I hate myself.

I love El Indio's mordiditas—taquitos cut up in bite-size pieces and covered in nacho cheese and jalapeños, with a side of classic El Indio chips—and goddamnit I hate myself.

What I love most if I'm anywhere near Clairemont is the chile relleno burrito from El Cotixan on Genesee. I go there late at night with Tyler or Joey Carr or Maggie, and sometimes everyone all at once, and like one pulsing, jittering body we order at the counter and sit down and wait for our food while Vicente Fernandez sings sentimental ballads over the speakers.

> *"Quisiera reventarme*
> *hasta las venas*
> *Por tu maldito amor*
> *Por tu maldito amor"*

At these moments, I don't hate myself, but I'm too caught-up to know—caught-up in talking about someone's shithead boyfriend who fucked a dancer from Déjà Vu or about so and so's meth problem and how it's destroying their face or what the hell was up with that stupid shitty band that opened for Tristeza last week at Scolari's?

Tyler sips his soda and tells Maggie and me about this jock douche in his class Big Todd Barkley who's a terrible homophobe. Tyler is the first person I've met who seems like both a boy and a girl. He's a glamrocker.

He makes it look good. He says, "I used a Sharpie and made this fake fraternity shirt with Greek letters that spell out F A G just to piss Big Todd off and freak him out."

Maggie laughs and takes Tyler's soda and sips it.

"Don't get murdered, Tyler," she says, but you can tell she's unworried. Tyler's the sassiest, toughest human I know, and I have no doubt he can take care of himself. At El Cotixan he orders a plain bean burrito. Maggie gets a potato burrito with extra sour cream and a side of chips. If Joey Carr comes along he doesn't eat that often because of all the crystal he smokes, but if he does he gets taquitos that come covered in shredded cheese, sour cream, guacamole, and diced tomatoes. For me it's the chile relleno burrito or nothing. Once they were out of poblano peppers and it ruined my life— until the next day, when I ordered two and ate both.

There is not much I love more than eating too much. I want to be a pig—a pig with its snout down in the trough, a pig rooting out truffles in some medieval forest, happy, gluttonous, because gluttony is what a pig loves most. Two of everything. Three on a good day. Disregard entirely how you will feel later. Eat joyously because to eat with a joyous heart is one of the greatest pleasures you will know.

When our order is called, Tyler gets up and grabs it for us and serves us like someone's nice mom.

Once he's set our plates in front of us, he gets us napkins then limes and hot sauce from the salsa bar. Like Chente, Tyler goes for the classic San Diego red. I like the mild green. Maggie doesn't take salsa.

"You guys okay?" he asks. "Need refills?"

"Thanks, Tyler. I'm good," says Maggie, unwrapping her potato burrito. "Don't you guys think 'potato burrito' sounds like 'Giovanni Ribisi'?"

I agree with Maggie then I tell Tyler I've got everything I need and that he's earning a great tip. He grabs my cup and refills my soda anyway.

Tyler is a pleasure to be around. It's a joy to be his friend and stand enshrined in his glamorous, elfin benevolence. Maggie is a wild animal, and in another life she would have hung out at Warhol's Factory and been a tough New York Italian kid writing a tell-all memoir at 18. Both have that brash, energetic carelessness you see only in teenagers, that don't-give-a-fuck that either turns to bad choices or mellows into a fine, righteous, ethical anger as you age.

We wear ratty black hoodies or we wear tattered housewife dresses or we wear jeans from the Target teen girls' section that are too tight or we wear a sweater with colorful stripes and a few band buttons pinned to it or a purple scarf wrapped loose around our neck or eyeliner or sparkly gold-fleck black nail polish. We have thick, uncombed hair and we dye it black because that is how it is supposed to be. We know how it's supposed to be because we have set standards. Drawn up laws. These laws are unspoken, but we are ruthlessly judgmental of those who fall outside of the boundaries unless they do so with style or bravery. If we decide you are a bad-ass you are exempt from all criticism.

The chile relleno burrito at El Cotixan is a roasted then lightly battered poblano pepper stuffed with jack cheese wrapped tight in an oversized flour tortilla with refried beans, cheese, and sour cream.

It's best to take a decent-sized bite and let the steam pour out, so it cools for a second then squeeze half a lime into it.

That is how you do it, and that is how not to hate yourself, or to forget that you do, or to ignore that voice telling you such awful things. Like die. Like you are ugly and stupid. Like everyone thinks you're a joke and is tired of you. Like you will never be anything no matter how hard you try.

TOMATO SANDWICH

Joey Carr at night puking violently onto a parking me-
ter. Joey Carr hungover in the afternoon, smoking a
cigarette, wearing a stained white ringer t-shirt with
"That's DOCTOR Pepper to you" in red and black letters. Joey Carr at dawn, the party winding down, and
he's in jeans and a denim jacket with a novelty sheriff's
badge pinned to it, and he's lost his shoes and one of his
socks. His black hair flops into his face as he straddles
the arm of a couch rolling a joint on the open pages of a
copy of *People* magazine, supremely high, eyes glazed in
slits, mumbling something about how any horse could
kick any US President's ass if it really wanted to.

Joey Carr and Maggie Harker—like sunlit children
running together on the sidewalk up ahead of us, laughing, delirious, while Tyler and I lag behind, talking. Joey
Carr, who ate a tomato sandwich every day for the en-
tirety of the time we were friends because he loved the
book *Harriet the Spy*, and because Harriet refused to
eat anything but tomato sandwiches. Our friendship—
just as painful, sad, and dramatic as the book. Joey's
life—painful, sad, and dramatic. Like maybe every life
at times—painful, sad, and dramatic.

At Joey's slum apartment he would shout to me
from the kitchen about the merits of the tomato sandwich while I drank wine from a jug, and while he made
one for himself or two if he were stoned. The week he
was given his eviction notice I came over hungry after
work, and he made me a tomato sandwich with all the
pride and excitement of someone cooking an eight-
course meal for their dearest, sweet love.

Joey and I weren't close. He was more a friend of
Chente and Tyler, but I liked him enough if he wasn't
obnoxious drunk or nervy on speed, and sitting in his
famously trashed apartment at the end of him living
there and getting a trademark Joey Carr tomato sandwich felt right in a very foundational way. Joey had a
blue and white striped kiddie suitcase turntable on the

floor in the middle of the room amidst all the crumpled pieces of newspaper and beer cans and bread crusts and tin foil meth pipes and cassette tapes and ashtrays. While he busied himself in the small attached kitchen I played songs from a stack of 7"s next to the record player. I played a Palace Music song, a Cat Power song, and both sides of a Minmae single, and then he was done.

Walking back into the room, smiling crazily, Joey gave me a plate with two sandwiches and sat down cross-legged in front of me, our knees nearly touching, taking half of one of the sandwiches and jamming most of it into his mouth.

"Sho guh," he said, so good.

I took a bite, and it was true. The Joey Carr tomato sandwich—a perfect thing. Nice sourdough, sour enough that it felt damp, a thick but not overapplied layer of mayo, and thin-sliced roma tomatoes with a little salt and pepper. The sandwich cut neatly in diagonal halves.

It was a sparkling, bright, living kind of taste—alive with the viny tang and musk of the tomato, the tomato brought further to life by the salt, and the mayo and the water of the tomato soaking just barely into the bread to give it a nice texture.

I told him so. Told him he'd made a perfect thing.

"Duh," he said, rolling his eyes happily then eating the last bite of his sandwich, chewing, saying, mouth crammed full, "Nuh wun e'er buhliefs me."

"No one ever believes me" made up a central part of Joey Carr's personality at the time. Likeable yet never popular. His voice soft, often drowned-out in conversation. He could be wild and reckless, but where people loved Chente at his most reckless, Joey's wild acts made you nervous. There was something unbelievable about him, as if he were living a lie and skating along through the day hoping no one noticed. But they did. They noticed (whatever it was they noticed, I never saw) and they chose to stay distant. They watched him from afar as if he were an unpredictable animal. They talked about his smallest actions, even if their own actions weren't all that far from his. They were wary of

Joey and of his mania and his appetite for hard drugs and his endless, gushing endorsements of the tomato sandwich. So, they kept him at a safe distance. Joey had a lot of acquaintances at the time and not many friends.

What unhappy people like most is to judge others who are doing the same things as them. They like to point at someone and whisper about how bad and awful and sinful they are because that person is doing exactly what they do and they can't come to terms with their own deeds. First stones cast, they talk and they judge and they damn their targets eternally. They damn them properly, righteously. They damn damn *damn* them, and *oh* it feels good. (I know how good it feels because I've done it too. I'm just as bad as they are.)

Thinking back on it, I see what a shame that was. Joey Carr and his tomato sandwiches and his crazed, hopeful exuberance were in no way bad. Joey was a Byronic sort of kid, and you felt he was doomed, marked for a dark and early end. But to push him away? That meant you missed out on something good, real, and true. Joey Carr wasn't living a lie. He lived how he wanted to live, and for anyone who has seen such a thing, it is a brave act to witness, even if the results aren't nice or healthy or pretty.

Not all true things are good and not all honest acts make your life better. Sometimes a true thing is ugly, mean, twisted-up, and corrupt. Sometimes honesty kills. Truth can be a knife cutting away the worthwhile parts of your life. Like a lot of us at the time, Joey Carr wanted desperately to die and sometimes when people see that they choose to hold you at arm's length rather than help. Why get close to the kamikaze pilot when you know his goal is to crash? Why care about the fire as the fire burns down?

Some people are rats watching other rats drown. They sit on higher ground, shaking their rat heads warily, saying in rat voices, "Well, they're drowning like we said they would. They shouldn't go ahead and drown if they didn't want to drown."

LAST YEAR'S HALLOWEEN CANDY

****

I'm sitting on the floor of Joey's apartment eating old Halloween candy while he smokes crystal on the couch. Joey cleaned the place spotless in order to move out then got a last-minute reprieve from his landlord. A week later it's trashed again. Piles of music magazines and copies of *SLAMM* and *the Reader*. Dirty clothes in heaps, pizza boxes, CDs, old beer cans for ashtrays, an empty jug of Carlo Rossi with a black and white bumper sticker stuck on it reading "I Love a Clean San Diego."

The big red plastic bowl of Halloween candy I found in his fridge is all mini bars. Mini Hershey's, mini Snickers, mini Milky Ways, mini KitKats. I unwrap a Hershey bar the size of a domino and stick it in my mouth as he tells me about stealing the bowl off someone's porch last year along with the yellow 3 x 5 card taped to it that reads: "Use the Honor System Please! Thanx! Happy Halloween!" with little drawings of bats, pumpkins, and spider webs all around the letters. I try not to think about this because thinking about it breaks my heart. It feels like kicking the hell out of someone's hope, pissing on someone's belief in how people can be generous and moderate and help each other out and not be such selfish assholes all the time. Sometimes I think Joey's half evil; that there is a fundamental piece in his heart that runs contrary to all that is good and sweet about him.

Last week Joey told me he felt like he was becoming a vampire, that a demon had crawled into him and had begun to slowly replace what was once Joey Carr with its own vile, diabolical self.

"The problem being," he said, "I think I like it more than I like the real me. Sometimes it feels better to be mean than nice or kind, and I like myself more when I'm an asshole to people. How fucked up is *that*?"

I open the thin, orange, crinkling package of a Kit-Kat as Joey, sitting cross-legged, runs his yellow Bic lighter under the bowl of his glass pipe. The rock inside begins to cook and turn black then white smoke swirls up inside the bowl like a genie and begins to trail out of the hole at the top in a thin, slow, ghostly wisp. When it does that, Joey drops the lighter on the cushion next to him, picks up the cut-in-half McDonald's straw balanced on his knee, and sucks the smoke into his lungs. He sucks in deep. Sucks in until his cheeks hollow out and until his eyes narrow to slits.

Still cross-legged, Joey lets himself fall backward on the couch, and he lies there holding the pipe and the straw clutched to his chest, worrying at them with his fingers, squeezing them rhythmically. "Shit," he says happily, "shit, shit, shit, shit." He keeps saying shit and it feels like he's not going to stop because it's a happy shit and I can tell it feels good to say shit and I can't blame him for wanting to feel good. "Shit," he says, and this shit seems like an impressed shit, like he's impressed at how high he is.

I unwrap a Milky Way and break it in half, stretching the caramel inside between the two parts. The caramel is beautiful—dark bronze, shining, and the light from the single window in Joey's apartment is dusty. It's the light of sunset, but here you don't see the sun or the sun setting. Looking out, you see the concrete staircase of the apartment on the second story, and the dust moving in the light—rising, falling, drifting lighter than air. Looking in, you see the ruined apartment and Joey on the couch. You see his gray skin. It's gray like turkey without gravy, like something dead with everything that makes it good cooked out of him. Joey looks like his own dead body, like his own extinguished twin, like a vision of his future.

"Shit," Joey says one last time then sits up and packs another bowl.

FISH SANDWICH

****

Joey says the first time he had a fish sandwich he was so stoned he sat in his truck at a stop sign waiting for the sign to turn green until three songs had passed on the radio. This was last week. The sandwich he remembers disappearing in his hands, vanishing in small bits like time lapse photography until there was nothing but a greasy paper-lined plastic basket, a thing of tarter sauce, and a few Lays chips. He tells me how he feels like he was cheating on tomato sandwiches by ordering it, but he was so high that any sense of allegiance was out of his hands.

He tells me the bun was soft, like a hamburger bun, grilled lightly in butter, mayo on the bottom half, and only enough tarter sauce on the inside top to give it a sharp vinegary edge; then a leaf of fresh butter lettuce folded in two, a large slice of tomato, salted and peppered, and the fish itself cut in a neat and tidy square, breaded in crunchy corn meal batter, with a slice of cheddar nearly melted but not so much as to be dripping or messy. He tells me it was the best sandwich he'd ever had only he was so high he doesn't remember where he got it and of course it being the best means he's desperate to find the place again. "It's somewhere in O.B.," he tells me. "Somewhere on Newport maybe."

Beyond that it's gone.

Joey's memory has become like filo dough—thin, flaky, breaks easy.

He's spent this past week selling heroin to people we know.

"Just this week then I'm out," he says, and, man of his word, he follows through.

At the end of the week, he's got more money than he's ever had (bills rolled and held secure with rubberbands in a shoebox under his couch).

He says, "The money. Just having it. God it feels wonderful. I don't want to spend it on anything. I just *want* it. Knowing it's there ... I feel so much safer. I like thinking about it. Imagining it under me as I sit on the couch," and I change the subject.

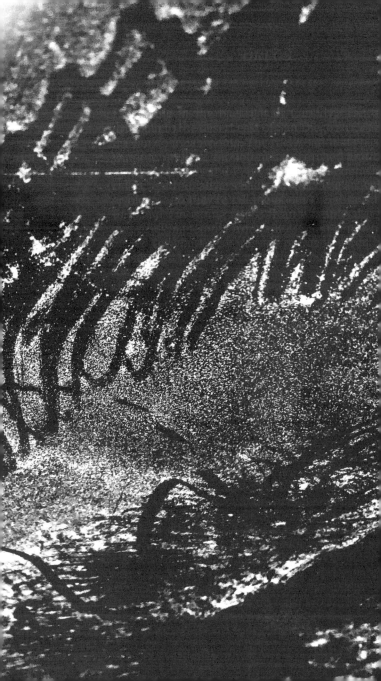

CROISSANTS

As I'm mopping up behind the serving tables after the dining room clears out, I eavesdrop on two of the bus-boys talking about croissants and a girl from the break-fast shift they call "the Breakfast Shift." I know her well. Her name is Cassidy Nguyen. Another new friend. Those close to her call her Lil' Cassidy. Lil' Cassidy's family is second-generation Vietnamese-American. Her mom died last year from breast cancer and her dad and brother are in the Marines up at Pendleton. She wants to open a florist's shop. She's 19 and she's working her way to it—living cheap in Golden Hill, saving her pay-checks, selling drugs on the side, staying in at night. Lil' Cassidy's a fighter—tough, mean, and sharp-edged like a piece of broken obsidian, but a real sweetheart. She's generous, energetic, loving. Huge fan of Lou Reed, ni-trous oxide, cocaine, movies involving disco clubs, and bubblegum ice cream. The day the Rite Aid in Hillcrest retired the flavor, she called in sick and that night we had a wake where we put blue makeup all over our faces and called ourselves the BFA (the Bubblegum Fucking Army) and got stumbling drunk.

Tonight's meal for the residents was prime rib, baked potato with sour cream and chives, apple sauce, and croissants. After our shift we're allowed to take as much as we want home, but half the time we eat while we're finishing our work. Those of us who do crystal, like most of the kitchen staff, and Joey Carr before he quit, don't eat at all. I eat voluminously, frantically, and I bring as much home as I can. My apartment fridge is jammed full of white styrofoam containers of work food with dates written in red Sharpie. Rice pilaf hard-ening to a block of yellow. Eggplant moussaka. Potatoes au gratin. Various casseroles. Potato pancakes. Things old people eat. Things you ate if you were a young adult during the Second World War. Some of the residents were in the Camps. You see numbers on their wrists and that's the only way you know. Those sweet, old,

Yiddish-speaking women (and only a few men) lived through things unimaginable. There's a woman here born in Auschwitz. Can you imagine it, and yet she still lives? Still laughs? Still sits down at dinner with a table of women (she's one of the younger ones) and talks and asks so and so to pass the salt or the butter or the basket of rolls. She exists. Everything about me feels flimsy and insubstantial in the face of that.

The busboys Shane and Patrick are wearing black pants and white button-up shirts, black bowties, and aprons stained with food and brown liquid. They're sitting on the linoleum floor behind the serving station with a basket of croissants between them and they're dipping them in a small white bowl of au jus as they talk. Shane and Patrick refer to each other and Shane's shitty cousin Super Brad as "the Irish Mafia." Super Brad worked with us until last month when he was fired for pissing into a pitcher of lemonade he planned to serve to the residents. They caught him on camera in grainy black and white—standing in the walk-in cooler, pissing happily into the pitcher, rapping soundlessly to himself, bobbing his head side to side, gesticulating wildly with his free hand.

Sitting on the floor, Shane tells Patrick, "Brah, last night the Breakfast Shift was on my lap all crazy and shit and she pulled off her shirt, and I held them lil' tiny titties in my hands and I's like, Hehhhhh-ells yeah, brah."

"Tight. Irish Mafiaaaaaah!"

"Yeah, brah. The Breakfast Shift was suckin' my dick like boom boom boom boom and I had them titties in my hands just like, Yeah yeah yeah yeah yeaaaaaaah whooooo's the kang?! Who's the KANG?"

"Crowsawnts is the *shit*."

"Guess who's back? Back again. Crowsawnt's back. Tell a fren!"

"You fuck her?"

"The Breakfast Shift? *Yeah*. She let me jizz on her face. Like, wham, yeeeeeah, brah!"

"Tiiiight. Irish Mafia, merrrfuckah."

"Ireeeesh Mafi-UH. Yeee-uh. You know! You know!"

Shane and Patrick do a handshake that includes a snap of their fingers at the end.

I know what they're saying isn't true because I went to the movies with Lil' Cassidy and Sara Rodriquez last night and because Lil' Cassidy does not like men in the way they think she does. Lil' Cassidy has been dating Sara since junior year of high school. Shane and Patrick know none of this because knowing things like this would put Cass and Sara in a bad position. Shane and Patrick are vehement, strident, violent homophobes. They're the kind of homophobes who talk about wanting to rape lesbians and shoot gay men. Would they do it? Does it matter? Talking about it is enough to make you irredeemable.

Shane and Patrick think Lil' Cassidy is Chinese just like they think all the Asian staff members are Chinese and all the Central and South American employees are Mexican. Half the kitchen staff is from Central America. Manuel the cook from Honduras. Alfredo and Memo the Panamanian dishwashers. A big group of the CNAs who work upstairs are Laotian. The dining room supervisor Robby is from the Philippines. To the Irish Mafia they're all Chinese and Mexican.

They continue:

"Brah, I's gonna fuck that little slut again this weekend. C'mere, the Breakfast Shift. C'mere, beeaaaawtch. Ride that Chinese wong tong chinga tang ass. Ride that tong chong ching ching ching ass! Yeah! Yeah! Yeah! Yeah! Boom! Boom! Boom!"

"You better or you're a fag."

"I'm takin' these crowsawnts home, brah."

"Bitch no you ain't. Half those is mine."

"Brah, I'm takin' these home because you ain't got a dick."

"Bitch, *I'm* taking those home because your ass is a fuckin' … a fuckin', like, your ass is a *pedophile*."

"Whas that? That mean gay?"

"It's what you are and it's why I'm taking them

home."

"Brah, whaaat?"

Tyler walks past pushing a bus cart and rolls his eyes at me and shakes his head. He hates Patrick and Shane more than anyone. I mouth the words, "Kill me," and put my hands around my neck like I'm choking myself to death, and he laughs as he takes the cart back to the kitchen. The Irish Mafia doesn't know what to think of androgenous, pretty Tyler.

When I finish cleaning up, I put the mop and the bucket away and grab a takeout box from the line and stuff it with croissants.

I fit as many as I can in there. Smash them flat. Press them together. A dozen. A few over a dozen. I get a second box and stuff it full and stick one last croissant in my mouth.

They're good croissants—flaky but not too dry, soft, buttery. At my apartment I'll mix up horseradish and mayo and use that for a dip.

The Irish Mafia are no longer in their spot.

They've left the empty basket and the bowl of au jus on the floor, but they're nowhere to be seen.

Something about the basket sitting there next to the bowl makes me profoundly sad.

I stare at the basket and the bowl, a big friend and a little friend left behind by two pieces of human trash, and I have to fight back tears.

The retirement home is on Mount Soledad.

Soledad means Loneliness or Solitude in Spanish.

Solitude Mountain.

The dining room is empty.

The other waiters have reset the tables, and the cooks have taken the metal serving tubs of prime rib to the back so the kitchen staff and the maintenance guys can get theirs.

Petra Cooper stands next to the rows of light switches on the far end of the dining room.

"James! You done?!" she shouts. She's tying her frizzy explosion of hair back behind her head. "Let's get outta here! I got homework!"

"I'm done! Later, Coop!"

"See ya tomorrow!"

I walk out as the lights shut off, starting in the back of the dining room and following me up to the front, clicking off louder and louder as they reach me.

When I step through the kitchen doors, I look back, and the dining room is dark.

SHEET CAKE

****

Last week I quit the retirement home and took a job at the new online version of the daily newspaper. Tonight we're celebrating and Lil' Cassidy says she's got a shopping list for our James-and-Cassidy-only party. The list is in the glove box, and I find it and read it aloud as she drives us down University to the sex shop. I'm drinking from my hey-you-quit-your-job present—a quart bottle of good tequila Cass gave me wrapped in a piece of newspaper. The radio is on and finally it's a song I like—John Doe and Exene from X singing about how the world's a mess, and I'm half-drunk with my saucy, mean, smart-ass friend on a warm San Diego night and all feels true and good.

"Sex shop. Nitrous," I read off the list. "What the fuck, Lil' Cass. You get creepier every day."

Lil' Cassidy and I are rude to each other. It's not a friendship I have with anyone else, but with her it's natural. When she's mean to me, I know she loves me, and when I'm mean to her, I can tell she feels appreciated. With her I'm someone else. Sometimes it's nice to be someone else. Especially when you don't like yourself. When you don't like who you are, being someone else is like taking a sweet, wonderful, relaxing vacation.

"James, I wanna blow my mind out on some nitrous and listen to Lou Reed," she says, turning the radio down as we slow to stop at a red light. "You can join me or keep bein' a little church lady bitch."

Cassidy tells me the sex shop in North Park is the best place to get the lipstick-size canisters of nitrous oxide and the balloons she'll use to huff it, and I tell her she's going to make herself even stupider than she already is.

Lil' Cassidy wears black jeans, white Converse, a dirty white tank top, and a black leather jacket a few sizes too small. Last week she shaved her head except for two locks that trail down her cheeks like sideburns. It looks good on her. Tough. Like she's going to stab somebody or sell you a stolen car.

Up next on the list is dinner. "Dinner. Ralph's. Sheet cake," I read. "Like a whole sheet cake?"

"Yeah, dude."

"Disgusting, Cass. I can't believe you."

"Bitch, it's fuckin' Friday night and we're celebrating your new job. Doubleheader of good times. Party city."

"And you want to ruin it."

"You got it, babygirl."

Lil' Cassidy's nickname for me is babygirl. I'm not sure why, but it's nice to have a nickname.

I slouch in my seat and sip the tequila then sit back up again, wedging the bottle between my thighs. "Let's hit up Valentine's. Get something *actual*."

"James Jackson Bozic, doing whippits and eating a sheet cake *is* actual. Check your priorities, fuckface. You need to learn how to party."

"Oh yeah? Do I, Cass?"

"James, the Vengabus is coming, and you don't want it to leave without you."

"The Vengabus should crash," I say.

"Whatever. You're boring. They wouldn't let you on anyway. Look, I think about eating, like … just eatin' a whole fuckin' grocery store sheet cake all the time and I never do it. Why not do something you want to do?"

"Because it's not even real cake?"

"It's real."

"Cass, it's like if real cake … like if real cake got super depressed and gave up and sat around in its pajamas all day, smoking weed, eating cold pizza, and watching a *Saved by the Bell* marathon."

"Okay, that sounds fucking awesome, and anyway sheet cake is the bomb. You buy it at the bakery counter and they'll write whatever you want on it. That's half the fun, babygirl. Don't even *talk* to me about dinner until your dinner's been a whole sheet cake with some cool-ass shit written on it. I'll have them write something on there like, 'It's Friday Night, Dickheads, Let's Get Fat.' Something bitchy."

"Cass, they won't write that. They'll haul you off to

prison where you deserve to be. I'll tell them to throw away the key. I'll have you tossed in Alcatraz, the fuckin' *Rock*. I'll call Nicolas Cage and Sean Connery and be like, 'Alright guys, listen up, whatever you do, don't break into Alcatraz and let Cassidy out, because she's a *menace*.' That's what you are, Lil' Cass, a menace."

"I know a girl who works the cake counter at Ralph's. We dated in sophomore year. Tonight's her shift. She'll let me do whatever I want. Bitch loves me. You know why?"

"Why?"

"You really wanna know?"

"Yeah, Cass. Why?"

"Because I'm the *best*."

I laugh. "Alright, last one on the list is Buy Magazines. Like what kind of magazines? Music magazines?"

"I don't care," she says. "I'll read any magazine. I'll read a surf magazine where a bunch of fucking bros talk about how much they love surfboards. A magazine about how to kick someone's ass."

"Since when are you super into magazines?"

"Last week when me and Sara did acid with Petra, in the middle of it all, I was like, Cassidy, girl, your whole life is utterly false, and your goals are out of whack. You want to open a florist's shop? Fuck no, you don't. Life's too fucking short, and you'll be dead in a few decades if you're lucky enough to make it that far. Why waste it running a fucking business that'll probably fail anyway? What you gotta do is work as much as you need at a shitty job like the retirement home, a place you don't give a fuck about, just to get by, and have a good time whenever you're not working. What's more important than having a good time?"

I tell her the flower shop idea is cool. That it would be nice to be surrounded by flowers every day. I remind her how much work she's put into it so far, how much she's saved up, all the research she's done, and the Learning Annex classes she's taking, the hours she spends with the *U-T*'s business section; how once she has her own company she won't have to answer to a boss like at the retirement home.

"Okay, dad," she says, "Look, I realized trying to do anything is a waste of time. Just do the bare minimum and spend the rest of your life having fun. Get high. Read a million magazines. Eat whatever you want. Eat a fuckin' sheet cake. Fuck as many people as you can before you die."

"Oh, I bet Sara *loves* that."

"Sara understands. I told her the next day. I was like, 'When we were on acid I realized I need to fuck more people.' She's cool with it."

"You sure about that?"

"I think so."

We pass rows of darkened storefronts, bright-lit gas stations, bars with people outside smoking. A cop pulls behind us and I stash the bottle of tequila under the seat. Cassidy lights a cigarette. The radio plays a horrible song about being a barbie girl in a barbie world. I turn it off and Cassidy says, "Bitch, what?" and turns it back on.

Back at Lil' Cassidy's apartment, I'm sitting on the floor drinking red wine from an old gallon-size pineapple juice can, flipping through a copy of *Spin* while Cassidy lies on her back on the mattress—high, head hanging over the edge, eyes shut.

"Muhfuckin' helicopters," she says, mumbling. "Buncha muhfuckin' helicopter-ass helicopters."

"Good. Now you have brain damage." I turn the page of the magazine in my lap. "This article talks about how Courtney Love used to work as a stripper in Portland."

"Courtney Love can do whatever she wants. I don't care."

"I guess it was before Kurt. You should read this article when I'm done, Cass."

"Yo, I'm sick of hearing about fuckin' Kurt Cobain. Kurt Cofuckinbain. My cousin named his pet snake Kurt Cobain. Kurt Cobain the pet snake. What an asshole."

"Your cousin or the snake?"

"Both. No one should have snakes as pets. It's like

living with the enemy. It's like living behind enemy lines."

"I'd lose my mind if there was a snake in my house."

"Sounds like there's helicopters in my head," she says. "Like whump, whump, whump. I feel like I'm in the war. I'd be a good soldier. If I cared about killing. I don't. Only person I'd kill is you. I'd kill your ass in a second and people would give me a medal."

The sheet cake is on the floor next to me with its plastic shell lid still on. Cassidy's too high to move, too high to eat or look at magazines.

Lil' Cassidy's studio apartment has a twin-size bed up against the wall and not much else. It's clean. Dark. Hardwood floors, the bed and a bedside lamp on a black-painted wooden end-table, a big rectangular cassette player radio from the '70s plugged in next to the wall, the stack of magazines, and the cake we bought. The door to the bathroom is shut and has a photocopied picture taped to it of Divine in *Pink Flamingos* pointing a gun at the camera. On the kitchen counter a stick of nag champa burns in its wooden holder.

"I'm trying this stupid cake," I tell her.

"Helicopters," she says. "The war. Kill you. Fuckin' medals. Medals all over my shirt. Be a *General* 'n' shit."

I snap the plastic shell off the top and set it aside. "This looks shitty for the record. For the record this sheet cake looks like the worst, stupidest thing I've ever seen." In pink icing the girl behind the counter has written, "My name is Lil' Cassidy. I am fake and a piece of trash." I run a finger along the edge and taste it. "Lil' Cass, this is crap. I was right. It tastes like dried-out toothpaste. Why is everything you like awful?"

"Hey sailor, put the Lou Reed on."

Put the Lou Reed on means put on Cassidy's tape of *Transformer*, the only record she ever listens to at home.

I set the cover back on the cake and crawl across the floor to her tape player.

"Where's it?"

"Bitch, it's *in*. Don't be dumb. It's *always* in. I thought we was friends, babygirl."

"You thought wrong."

"I forgot. You don't have friends because your ass is too ugly. James, you should be shot for being so ugly. They should throw you up against a wall and shoot you. Verdict, too ugly says the jury of your peers and the judge. Judge fuckin' *Wapner*. Judge fuckin' *Judy*. Fuck yeah. *All* the fuckin' judges up in this shit. A *judge* party. Show up at 10."

I flip the tape over and hit Play.

The music starts and now Lil' Cassidy is singing along. Her voice is better than Lou's. It's hoarse and soft and husky.

"Vicious
You hit me with a flower
You do it every hour
Oh, baby, you're so vicious"

I sit up against the wall by the boombox and close my eyes and listen to her sing the next three songs. She mumbles through the fourth track then stops and that's when I realize she's asleep.

OREOS

I'm sitting in the backseat of Cassidy's car while we drive out to the desert east of San Diego so Cass and Petra can do mushrooms. The rocky sandflats pass by the window, endless, monotonous, scorched and baked to nothing. Cassidy and Petra are talking about what Petra calls Cassidy's "always bad attitude." The air-conditioner blows and they're talking about the always bad attitude and I'm eating Oreos from a family-size package and drinking tequila from a Boy Scout canteen. Before we left the apartment Cassidy put neon green and pink makeup on us. Stripes across our cheeks like new wave idiots.

Petra, sitting in the passenger seat, says, "Cass, the problem is ... is you're so negative."

"How am I so negative?"

"You know how you're negative."

"Seriously, like enlighten me."

"Cass, you hate *everything* and you never say anything positive about—"

"I say positive shit."

"See, Cass, right there. It's positive *shit*. It's not, 'I say positive *things*.' It's positive shit. See how you're framing this? Positivity is, to you, shit. You're making my argument for me."

"Whatever. I'm fun."

"You being fun isn't up for debate, Cass. Being fun doesn't mean you're not a dick. You can be a total hateful downer and be fun at the same time."

"So I'm a downer now."

"That's just an ... I'm just using that as an example. I say the word 'You,' but I mean everybody. Anybody can be a total downer and still be fun. I'm using the universal You."

"I'm just as nice as anybody else, Petra. No one's fuckin' positive all the time. That would be oppressive as *shit*. People who are nice all the time are oppressive and stupid. You can't trust them."

"How so?"

"You can't trust them because everyone's got a mean side. People who are nice all the time are hiding it. They go home and kick their dog. They tie up their wife and beat the hell out of her. No one is nice all the time. You try to be nice all the time and you bottle that shit up? Nah, you're gonna fuckin' snap at some point. Go postal. Fuckin' shoot your neighbor for playing their music too loud."

"Cass, pause for a sec. Let's play a driving game."

"Okay."

Petra looks at me in the rearview. "James. You down?"

I tell her no, I am not. No driving games.

"Alright, Cass. It's just me and you. I'm going to say a bunch of things and I want you to tell me if you like them, love them, or hate them."

"I feel like you're setting me up for failure here, but yeah, sure, let's play your stupid game."

"Alright, Cass. Doctors."

"Hate."

"Why?"

"Everyone hates doctors. Going to the hospital is never good. You don't go to the doctor because you're feeling great. You only like doctors if they're giving you good news. Fuck doctors. I don't trust them anyway. They're all sadists and twisted liars."

"The San Diego Zoo."

"Like."

"Really?"

"You're right. Hate. Fuck the Zoo. The Zoo's depressing."

"SeaWorld."

"Super hate. You know the killer whales rape each other, right?"

"What? No, they don't."

"Remember when I broke my toe? I went to this sports medicine guy in La Jolla my dad uses. He was having a bad day or something and he kinda, like, broke down and lost his shit. Told me how he's the doctor for the SeaWorld trainers and that the killer whales are all insane. They beat each other up. They form rape gangs. They're totally fuckin' crazy and violent. He said the trainers get hurt all the time and you never hear shit about it because SeaWorld keeps it quiet. Besides Captain Kid's World, SeaWorld is the worst kind of no. I'd let all the crazy, fucked-up whales out into the sea and burn that place *down*."

"How about the doctor?"

"The sports medicine guy?"

"Yeah. How about him?"

"Yeah, Dr. Dipshit. He was a douche. Smelled like McDonald's fries."

"That's not a bad smell. McDonald's fries are great."

"They are, but I mean, like, old ones. Like maybe you got McDonald's last week and ate it in your car then locked the car up with half the food still in the bag during a heatwave and for days it just dried and got all fuckin' desiccated and stale. Old fast food car smell."

"So hate?"

"Hate."

"Okay, work."

"Work?"

"Our job."

"Oh, absolute hate. Fuck that place. They should go out of business. I'll go work for James' newspaper. Go *investigate* some shit."

"Okay, next, um, San Diego."

"Petra, that's not fair."

"That's not fair how?"

"No one loves their hometown."

"I do," says Petra. "San Diego's dope. Right, James? San Diego? Dope?"

Petra looks at me in the rearview for support.

"Yeah," I say. "It's alright. It's a good town except the fancy parts."

"No way," says Cass. "Hate, hate, hate. Nuke it. Call a Russian up and be like, *Send me some nukes, man*."

"Strangers."

"Hate."

"Mormons."

"Hate."

"Jehovah's Witnesses?"

"Special hate. I see 'em riding their bikes around the neighborhood and I wanna hit them with my car. I know what you did last summer, bitches. *Smack* into my bumper. Right over the hood. Witness *that*, bitch. Witness me *killing* your ass. Go write a *bible* about it."

Petra, laughing, shaking her head, says, "You're a monster. You know that?"

"Yes. I do."

"Okay, next. Uh, like, men who wear shorts."

"Look like giant toddlers. Hate."

"People who wear sandals."

"Don't ever wear shoes you can't get chased in if the occasion were to arise. Hate."

"Turtlenecks."

"Hate. Unless you're French then you're cool."

"Lou Reed."

"Hate."

"*Cass*, he's your favorite artist."

"Hate him because he sucked after *Transformer*."

"People who wear colorful clothes out at night."

"Come on. You know this already. We've talked about that one. This is a set-up."

"It is a set-up. But for argument's sake."

"Hate."

I snap off my seat belt and lean up between the two front seats. "Oreos," I say, handing Petra the package.

"There!" says Cassidy, slapping her hand on the steering wheel. "*Thank* you! Right there! I love Oreos. There is absolutely nothing to hate about Oreos. Oreos are perfect. Eating Oreos is you experiencing perfection. *See*, I like things."

I sit back in my seat and unscrew the first of three Oreos I've kept. My trademark way is I turn the cookie sides in opposite directions from each other, then open them carefully, slowly, so both parts have white stuff. After that I drag my teeth across each side, scraping away the filling. I eat the cookie halves next. The first then the second.

Petra says, "Let's do the mushrooms now so we're feelin' it by the time we hit the Castle."

The Castle is a rock formation Petra has been telling us about. A rock that looks like a castle, a cave at the bottom of it, ancient drawings on the cave walls.

Cassidy agrees, tells her yes, emphatically yes, and Petra opens the glove box and takes out a Ziplock bag of mushrooms. They each eat a few caps and don't offer any to me because they know I'll decline.

After that Petra lights a joint and rolls down her window.

"This is gonna be fuckin' sweeeet," Petra says just short of singing the words.

Cassidy turns on the car radio and it's her CD of Black Sabbath's *Paranoid*. It picks up right where we left off listening yesterday:

"All day long I think of things
But nothing seems to *satisfy*"

"Turn that shit *up*," says Petra in a fake deep voice like a bro, before taking a drag off the joint, holding it in.

Cassidy twists the volume and it's deafening, the bass shaking the thin metal panels of the car.

I take off my seatbelt again and lie on my back and sip the Boy Scout canteen of tequila while the hot air buffets through the cab, blowing our hair.

The song ends and Cassidy says, "Start the CD over. Let's hear the whole thing."

We drive in silence. The hot, dry air beating against us from the open windows.

We listen to "War Pigs," "Paranoid" again, "Planet Caravan," "Iron Man," and "Electric Funeral."

When the tequila is gone, I drop the canteen on the floor, sit up in my seat, and eat the last two Oreos. These I take in two bites. No strategy there. Just bite then bite. The soft cream and the dry cookie. Perfect.

Petra pulls off her shirt and bra and lets them fly out the window and then she's sitting with her feet up on the dash, frizzy hair blowing around her face as she packs a bowl of hash in Cassidy's pipe.

I can smell Petra's sweat. It's bad. Oniony. Not a

good smell.

Petra drops her feet from the dash, sits hunched forward, and takes a hit.

The music is a jet plane, a god's voice, an overcast dirge.

Petra sits back in her seat and blows her hit out the window. "*Mi* castle, *es su* castle," she says to herself, staring out at the desert, squinting.

Cassidy drives with one hand and unbuttons the top two buttons of Petra's corduroy pants then slides her hand down the front.

Petra sits up straight. "Damn, dude. Okay."

"This alright?"

"It's ... yeah. Yeah, keep going."

"I wanta make you come right when the mushrooms kick in."

"Okay," says Petra quietly, eyes closed now. "I'll tell you when to speed up when it starts to hit. But ... yeah, like, go slower."

"Like that?"

"Yeah, ughh," says Petra, holding onto the handle above her car door with both hands, her left arm in front of her face. "Like that."

I look away, out the window, out through the smudgy glass. The desert racing by. Tan, almost yellow, gray. The sky pale blue and not a cloud for miles. Not a cloud in all the world.

WENDY'S FROSTY WITH FRIES

****

Tyler's trying to quit meat, but he's been eating the spicy chicken sandwich at Wendy's all his life, and he loves shouting "SPICY CHICKEN ONLY LETTUCE!" into the menu speaker in a weird, made-up accent that sounds like a kid and also an angry old woman. I can't tell if yelling at Wendy's is his one outlet for meanness or if he's just excited about the sandwich. We sit in the drive-thru waiting for our food and Tyler lights a menthol and takes a drag before ashing out the window with a dainty flick of his wrist.

We're meeting Joey Carr and Lil' Cassidy at Belmont Park in Mission Beach. Joey wants to ride the Giant Dipper rollercoaster and Lil' Cassidy and Tyler love the pinball arcade and the bumper cars. I'm along for the ride. The amusement park makes me sad in a way I can't articulate. I know what'll happen is all the people having fun will overwhelm me and I will wander off while my friends play. I'll sit on the seawall and watch the ocean then I'll start feeling left out. By the time I feel left out, it'll be too late and too awkward to go back and join them. It's a bad situation I keep putting myself in, but I don't know how to stop.

Tyler unwraps his spicy chicken only lettuce with one hand as he drives and it's a catastrophe because there's no lettuce and they gave him a ton of mayo. Tyler hates sauce. Anything white and creamy he can't handle. It makes him insane.

"I can't *believe* these people," he says. "I'm calling Wendy when we get to the park."

"I didn't know you knew Wendy. That's cool."

I've got a Wendy's Frosty between my knees and I'm dipping my fries in it. The sweet and salty combination is magical. The Frosty is listed on the menu as chocolate, but it's actually chocolate and vanilla. Chocolate and vanilla can be best friends like sourdough and butter if it's done right. The Wendy's Frosty is done right. It's perfect like Oreos and Black Sabbath's *Par-*

anoid. Perfect like the best day of your life when everything goes right and you don't have to work and no one is upset with you.

The freeway at night is yellow-lit and colorless and not as crowded as it is in the day. We move effortlessly, weaving in and out of the lanes in Tyler's metallic blue Miata.

Tyler has his favorite CD in. *Happy 2b Hardcore Chapter 3: 15 Happy Hardcore Breakbeat Techno Anthems.* The music sounds like a Chipmunk's song in triple time—speedy, tinny-voiced samples of R&B singers, the beats micro-condensed into rapid-fire patters as the singer sings:

"Like a shooting star
Across the midnight sky,
Wherever you are
You're gonna see me fly"

Tyler says, "Actually I *do* know Wendy and I'm going to *ruin* her."

Tyler can be flip and cutting like Lil' Cassidy, but it's never about important things. He has a rule against hurting anyone's feelings.

"Well, before you get down to business, tell her the fries were great tonight," I say. "Tell her she did a good job on them and that she should keep doing whatever she did tonight. She's got the recipe dialed-in. Be like, Okay, Wendy, I got some good news and some bad news. Which you wanna hear first?"

"Nope. Sorry, James. Wendy is getting nothing but the bad Tyler tonight. Wendy's gonna curse the day she fucked with Tyler Monahan."

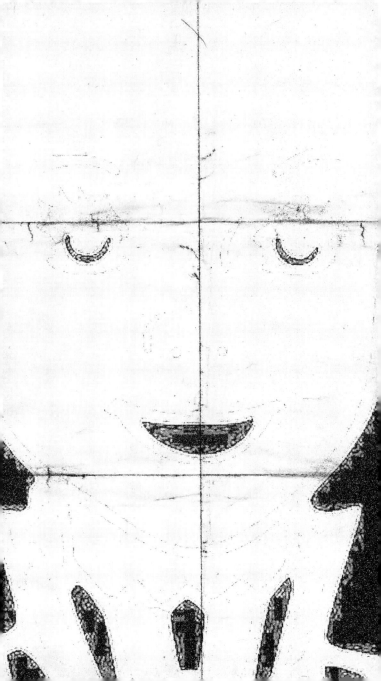

BOX BROWNIES

****

Cassidy says she drove out to the Salton Sea the week her mother died and did acid under a full moon then woke up in an abandoned car after having zero epiphanies about life, god, and/or death. Cassidy says it's fine that I'm not hateful anymore because she's got enough hate in her to go around. Cassidy says she hates cops, women who wear sweatpants, our friends Ted Boone, Ben Frank, Davy Ramos, my ex Julia and her cousin Laci, the Irish Mafia and the actual Mafia, Joey's ex Nicole and her best friend Darcy, men who wear baggy shirts that look like tents, this sketchy East County gem dealer both our dads knew called Severon Burgoon, everyone on television without exception, surfers, jocks, poker players, people who have rowboats ("get a fuckin' *motor*, dumb-ass"), and anyone who works at the P.B. Buffalo Exchange especially Lucy Keller whom I've never heard of until now. Apparently, Lucy Keller's "an absolute cunt who should be thrown off a cliff or smashed with a rock." Cassidy says she hates Joey Carr sometimes when he's sad and pitiful, me when I'm being a little baby, her dad, especially her dad, and nearly everyone else in her family for the way they handled her mother's death. Cassidy says she doesn't hate Tyler or Maggie. Maggie she says is the ultimate rock 'n' roll bad-ass. Tyler she loves and could never say a cruel thing about even in jest. Cassidy says Tyler should stop being a boy and commit to femininity because he makes it look so good all the girls she knows are jealous. Cassidy says she's done lusting after Petra Cooper because Petra is horribly straight and will never understand her. Cassidy says she's never doing cocaine again because meth lasts longer and is easier to find and people don't romanticize it like they do coke, and fuck romantics anyway. Cassidy says she's judgmental of everyone, but romantics get it the worst, second only to people who wear large sneakers that make their feet look abnormally big or men with small ponytails. Cassidy says her mother was the only romantic she never judged because her mother's romanticism was tinged with a sadness so sharp it cut into every aspect of her life. Cassidy says when her mother was alive she (her mother) would make Ghirardelli box brownies and they would sit on the couch together and eat the whole pan. The trick is if they're not chewy throw the whole thing away. Chuck it in the trash like a rotten fish. From the box is fine, but use an extra egg, she says, and don't cook it all the way. You want it fudgy, dense, not light and cakey. Cassidy's mom's brownies were a ritual when Cassidy's dad was deployed. During Desert Storm they didn't hear from him for two weeks, and they ate brownies every night. Every night a pan of them and the usual spot on the couch and they'd eat and watch anything but war coverage. Anything but CNN and Wolf fucking Blitzer and his terrible old man baby face Cassidy wanted to kick like a soccer ball. They watched Urkel make a guest appearance on *Full House* and that was exciting. They watched *Davis Rules* and they watched nature documentaries on PBS. When they ran out of things to watch they played VHS copies of their comfort movies. *Adventures in Babysitting* and brownies. *City Slickers II: The Legend of Curly's Gold* and brownies. *Kindergarten Cop* and brownies. *Revenge of the Nerds II: Nerds in Paradise* and brownies. Cass and her mom watched *Nerds in Paradise* three times. Three times *Nerds in Paradise* and three pans of brownies. Three pans of brownies and thrice the Tri-Lambs chased by alligators wearing nothing but their underwear. Three pans of brownies and three times Lewis punching frat villain Roger in the jaw at the end and Roger falling into the pool three times like a frat villain should.

EGGS FLORENTINE
****

Tyler says he and Petra saw a dead man at the retirement center today. "Right before the lunch shift," he says, as we sit on the seawall watching the ocean tossed by wind—gray and stormy. He smokes a menthol slowly with all the smoldering drama and style of a 1940s movie starlet, and tells me how they were setting up the coffee stations on the west-side serving line when they heard sirens and rushed to the window. Two of the CNAs from upstairs had the man on a stretcher outside the front entrance and Tyler and Petra watched from the second-floor windows as the ambulance crew took their time loading him in. The wind blowing the palm trees. The sky bright gray. Tyler says he was dead already, his mouth open, the shape of a kidney bean, the shape of a cartoon character's mouth when they're crying, his face as gray as the overcast sky. Somebody's grandpa, somebody's best friend, somebody's lover, dad, enemy, uncle, worst nightmare, safe haven, tyrant, place to find hope, who knows, just *somebody*. Tyler says his head flopped side to side, his old man white hair blowing in the breeze while they loaded him in, and then they shut the doors of the ambulance and the CNAs and the EMTs stood having a cigarette. The meal that morning was eggs florentine, side of either bacon or sausage links, your choice of toast. Tyler with pink and silver glitter on his cheeks, a new Ziggy Stardust hairdo, wearing a sheer mesh tanktop, and shiny silver pants says, "What the fuck is eggs florentine anyway?"

BURRITOS, VARIOUS

****

Tyler thinks Maggie is hooking up with Joey Carr. I don't say anything because I know it's true. Tyler still loves Maggie and I think Maggie loves Tyler, but Maggie is growing up. She's changing, searching for different things than what she wanted before. Tyler is casually, shallowly in love or possibly lust with Petra Cooper, but Petra's dating Cassidy now. Tyler's also in love with this rich girl Hanna Meyer who lives in a mansion up on Mount Soledad. We go to Café Crema or 976 together, and he helps Hanna with her chemistry homework, but Hanna's world is a different world than ours. Hanna's parents are in Monaco this month buying art. Her house has a clay tennis court and a hot tub with a view of the sea. The house is all glass and steel and there's a Basquiat in the foyer with a row of spotlights below it. (There's a *foyer*. That's enough to show the difference between Hanna's life and ours.) Hanna's dad was friends with Keith Haring and Kenny Scharf, went to Rothko's studio as a child, saw *No. 61* in progress. Hanna's mom is a Fluxus artist and once threw a drink on Charles Bukowski for saying creepy shit to her.

Hanna Meyer is an art world thoroughbred and a pegasus with gossamer wings and we're ratty mules standing in the mud waiting for an apple. Tyler's lonely and I'm lonely and we hang out a lot and go to bars that take his fake ID—Tobacco Rhoda's or Zara's or the nameless bar on the edge of the Gaslamp where you can pay to have sex with the girls who work there. That's something neither Tyler nor myself would do, even though we like the romance of drinking somewhere so rowdy and lawless. Maybe Joey Carr would. Joey thinks differently than we do, or maybe we just think he does. Joey's a hard read sometimes. Tough but mostly fronting, careless but concerned with every small detail and riddled with worries like tiny, chewing ants.

Joey's not returning Tyler's calls because he's with Maggie all the time. I asked Maggie once if Tyler was in love with Joey and she laughed and said Tyler's too complicated to follow sometimes but maybe, probably a little? Tyler and I get burritos then drive down to Ocean Beach and walk out onto the pier to eat them. Whenever Tyler's sad, I advise food because food is what works for me. Food is the greatest drug of all time and a proper bandaid. It's a hug when you need it, a way to forget your problems and blot out the noise in your head. Cassidy calls me "Miss Fat Lady" because of that, and it hurts my feelings and when it hurts my feelings she calls me "Miss Fat Lady Sad-Feelingsworth, of Cry County Isle." Cassidy's a dick when your defenses are down. Tyler's not and hanging out with him feels safe and healthy. He'll never make you feel bad. He's too kind, too pure of heart. Tyler's like a neon, campy Mister Rogers or a glamrock Levar Burton. Tyler makes sense to me, and I think I make sense to him too.

Years later I learn from a mutual friend that Tyler never cared about food. For Tyler, food was a nuisance, a chore—he ate because it's something you have to do to survive. He took no pleasure from it. Not like me. Tyler played along when I tried to use eating as a tactic to cheer him up, but he wasn't doing it for himself. It was for *me*. To make *me* feel better. Food didn't help Tyler, but he never let on. He knew it helped me and that me helping him (or me *trying* to) helped me as well. That was a gift of love he gave me, a gift I didn't know I was getting.

Out at the end of the O.B. pier, the ocean moves beneath us, the water deep green, and the waves crashing against the pilings with a spray of white foam. Surfers float sitting on their boards in their black wetsuits. Seagulls perch on the white-painted railing watching us eat. Old men fish, standing next to plastic buckets of their doomed catch. Tourists snap photos of the hazy coastline. My burrito is beans, rice, and guacamole. Tyler's is plain beans. We lean against the railing and we eat while the sea breeze blows our hair back from our faces and just now everything is right and nothing hurts at all.

Just now.

SUB SANDWICHES

****

After I get off work at the internet newspaper, Lil' Cassidy and Joey Carr and I put on wigs and drive down to the harbor. Cassidy's aunt Linh worked at Ken's Wig Shop in City Heights and when they fired her she broke in one night and filled the back of her Honda with stolen product. Cass took a box of them labeled "platinum blondes" from her aunt's place last week as payment for helping Linh move from Sherman to Golden Hill.

Cass, Joey, and I in our long blonde Ken's Wig Shop wigs are sitting on a bench down at the harbor with a bag of sub sandwiches, watching the lights of the boats. A few weeks ago, Cassidy and Joey met a kid up in Oceanside who sells coke and they have been on a shithouse of a bender. I talked them into eating because I'm scared of how thin they're getting, how hollow their cheeks are. They've been calling in sick to work. Sitting around Cassidy's place shooting up speed and cocaine, listening to the Lou Reed tape, talking around the clock. Joey and Cass have been hanging out a lot and now they're even dressing alike. Black jeans, tight leather jackets, dirty t-shirts. Tonight is their first night out of the apartment in days. They smell like sick sweat and they look like ghouls. Not in a good way. Not like romantic ghouls. Like ghouls who are ghouls because they've been starved in a prison camp, like they've had pneumonia for a decade.

The harbor is beautiful at night. The black, shining water. The lights of the docks and the dark boats sitting still like they were put up for bedtime and now dream of the sea and friendly whales. Cassidy and Joey are talking about themselves. Cassidy talks for a while about herself. Joey talks about himself. Then they trade off. I sit in the middle and drink from a quart bottle of tequila in a brown paper bag and listen. The drunker I get the less I worry about them. The drunker I get the less I moralize. *Now* they're pretty. *Now* they're the right kind of ghouls. Now they're doing nothing wrong

163

at all. I love them and I don't care. So what if my friends are shooting up all day and turning into skeletons? So what if they're doing something that will very much kill you? So what, so what.

Now I'm drunk and the world is soft and gauzy and cute. You (yeah, you reading this) you're cute. They're cute. I'm cute. We're all a bunch of cotton candy clouds of nothin'-matters-at-all.

Cassidy says, "Sara was like, '*Yo*, if you want to see other people you should go see other people, Cass, because this ain't what I want from life, this shit's what *you* want, this is your new thing, and I'm a) not getting in the way of your new thing and b) it's disrespectful to me, Cass.' So, I's like, Beee-itch, seeee ya, and it's been the Summer Olympics up in this shit ever since. You flimsy-ass baby ladies wouldn't be able to handle it. This level of vigorous, sustained fun would destroy most people, but I'm cruising along like fuckin' row, row, row your boat fuckin' gently down the fuckin' stream. I was made for this. Merrily, merrily, merrily. Life is but a dream, muhfuckers."

Joey says, "Ugh, my uncle used to tell me, 'You're too short to ever get fat. If you ever got fat you would look like a midget, you know that?' It hurt my feelings like a *sonofabitch*. I mean, he said worse things to me, but that really stuck in my head. I was like 12 when he said that. Twelve years old, can you believe that? What kind of person says that to a *child*? My-uncle-kind-of-person is who. He and my aunt could die tonight and I wouldn't even change facial expressions. I'd just be like, What? What happened? Oh, they died? That's it? That's *all* you had to tell me? Oh well. I'm so glad I'm here with you guys. I wouldn't wanna be anywhere else. Nowhere else. Just here. Right here." Joey has tears in his eyes. He wipes his face with the sleeve of his replica Lil' Cassidy leather jacket. "Just here. Right here. *Man*, I am fucking *high* right now." He laughs. "Oh shit. I am SO high. Ugh, whoa. That got on *top* of me."

I can't get a word in. That's okay. They're happy. Maybe they're happy for an artificial reason, a bad reason, but their happiness itself is real, and it's a nice thing to be around happy people—smiling Cassidy in her blonde wig, drumming the palms of her hands against her thighs as she talks about having sex with Petra Cooper. "Yo, first time I licked her pussy I made that muhfucker come in like a *minute*. She was like a rodeo horse. That shit made me feel like a *god*. Feels so good having that kind of power over somebody. Is that bad? I don't mean it in a bad way. Shit. Tell me if that makes me a bad person. I can't even tell. Fuck. Wait. Am I a *bad person*?" She stops talking, and now she's braiding one side of her blonde wig, fingers working furiously, nervously. "How do muhfuckers do a braid *anyway*?"

Joey—pale, haunted, shaky, all hard edges and angles like he's made of irregular panes of glass stacked together. His hands are waving in front of him to illustrate his point, as he tries to convince us whiskey is healthy. "It's the alcohol. You know, like, how in the Middle Ages people hardly ever drank water? Just beer or ale or whatever? Like fuckin' ale—ale, ale, ale all day because the water was contaminated with shit or whatever and the alcohol killed the bacteria and made it safe. Whiskey has such strong alcohol content that it gets in your stomach and kills off anything that might harm you. It cleans you out. It's like antibiotics, and I'm very careful, about the doses I mean. I'm taking care of myself. I saw a book about this at B. Dalton's written by a professor or a scientist or something. I think my parents would be proud of me. I think they'd get it." He pulls off his wig and rakes his nails across his scalp. "This shit is itchy. Is you guys' shit itchy from the wigs?"

Joey's parents were killed in a car accident when he was a few years old. He's obsessed about whether or not they would like him. All he has of his parents is a half-burned diary from his dad and fifty pages of a memoir his mother was working on at the time of her death. He digs through these for clues, for a sign that they would like him, that they would be proud of him. Last week on liquid ephedra and Mini Thins Joey told me his whole life story and did a dramatic reconstruction of his parents' relationship and his life up until now. We set up my tape recorder and filled 11 tapes with it. Eleven hours of Joey Carr and Joey's dead parents. He wants to do another session during Christmas break and he wants me to turn it into a novel.

Cassidy says, "Petra can't give head worth a shit because I'm the first girl she ever fucked, but I'm teaching her. Yo, I'm like *Mr. Holland's Opus* up in this shit and I'm gonna turn her ass into a *pro* and she'll thank me later. First time Petra went down on me it was like muh-fucker was lickin' an ice cream cone on a hot day, like she had to finish it before it melted. I's all, Nope, noooo, sit cho ass down in front of the chalkboard, Petra. I'm gonna get all Jaime Escalante *Stand and Deliver* on you."

Joey, sidetracked, sings, "The Bob Baker Auto Group where it's soooo nice to be niiiice. You guys remember that commercial?" He sings, "Highway five on Mission Bay Drive! Pacific Nissan!" and he sings, "At Pearson Ford we stand alone at Fairmont and El Cajon!" He says, "I always come back to that and—" clearing his throat, then singing "there's nnnnnever any glitter just value at Jerome's! There's nooo plaaace like *Jerome's*! One time my aunt and uncle actually *went* to Jerome's to buy a dresser and there was a fuckin', like, a fuckin' life-size cardboard cut-out of Jerome right when you walked in! I wanted to steal that shit. If I was Ben Frank I would. To have a fucking cardboard Jerome in your apartment when you came home would be so fucking nice. I would *honor* that shit. *Worship* that fucking shit. *Pray* to it. Ugh, man, I am so fuckin' high right now. Ughh. Cass, are you this high? I feel great."

After a while they slow down and stop talking and we sit and eat our sub sandwiches in silence. I stare out across the black, glossy baywaters—the breeze of the harbor cool on my face, the lights of the boats twinkling merrily, merrily, merrily.

My sandwich is on good, soft French bread. It has mayo, mustard, the smallest bit of Italian dressing, salt and pepper, three kinds of sliced cheese (cheddar, provolone, and swiss), avocado, sliced black olives, tomato, and just enough shredded lettuce for crunch. It's sat a while in the bag on the drive here and the mayo and dressing have soaked into the bread enough to make it doughy but not so much that it's a mess. You taste the tang of the mustard first, then the tomatoes, then the cheese. It comes to you in quick, distinct stages. The combination of all the ingredients is a lovely example of chemistry at work. The right things in the right amounts working together like a brave little team. My only regret is I should've ordered two.

Joey wraps his sandwich back up and sticks it in the bag. He's taken two bites. Not great. But it's something.

I finish my sandwich then get up and walk across the wet grass to the black ironwork railing that overlooks the baywaters.

"You better not go off and write some shitty-ass, wimpy poetry, you little bitch!" Cassidy shouts.

"Don't listen to her!" yells Joey. "Write that shitty-ass, wimpy poetry!"

As I walk, I lift both hands and give them a double middle-finger, which really means I love you, thank you, thank you for being here, thank you for being my friends because shit is so ugly and hard and ridiculous and sad. Thank you. That's what it means, thank you.

I take my wig off and stuff it down the front of my t-shirt like I'm pregnant with hair, and I stand at the railing, leaning my elbows on it, eyes shut. I hear the sound of Joey and Cassidy talking behind me, indistinct now, and the lapping of the baywaters against the concrete barrier, the hulls of the boats knocking gently against their moorings.

I listen to the sound of the harbor for a while then turn around and walk back to my friends.

EGGPLANT PARM

After work, in the tiny kitchen of my apartment, I make mac and cheese and talk to Chente on the phone. He tells me he's quit eating meat for good and I tell him I have too, and he says, "Oh shit, homie! They have a *soy* version of chorizo now! What?!" I tell him that's gross and there's no way that would ever work. "Listen, homie," he says. "You're about to get an education from the true-player-for-*real*." Chente explains how it does in fact work, as I rip open the blue and yellow cardboard box of mac and cheese, pull out the dry cheese powder, and dump the pasta in the water, the steam on my face flushing my cheeks.

Chente's still talking about how to prepare a good chorizo burrito the soy way as I dump the cooked noodles in the strainer then they're back in the pot with a half stick of butter, a little milk, and the powdered cheese. Looking at the rest of the butter in its greasy sort-of-paper sort-of-plastic wrapping I think *Fuck it* and put the other half in with the noodles. Full stick of butter. Here we go.

I stir the butter, milk, and cheese with the noodles as Chente talks about working in Mexican restaurants in New York City, and how sometimes he's the only Mexican in the place. "James, you know how I hate fake shit like that." I tell him I know exactly how he hates fake shit. "Drives me crazy," he says, and over the phone lines I can imagine him shaking his head. I hoist myself up onto the counter and eat from the pot with my wooden stirring spoon while Chente talks. He's excited about his new life. The crowded streets he takes to the subway where he plays guitar and sings ragtime blues for tips. The chill of late-afternoon in Manhattan, and the snow falling gently as seen from the windows of cafés and bagel shops, and you almost hear a lone saxophone playing nostalgically it's so New York.

He talks about the skyscrapers high above in the gray sky, and the basement bars, and Italian restaurants in the Village with a big plate of gnocchi with garlic butter sauce, and everyone going everywhere all at once, and you're so small and anonymous nothing matters, and *god* the immensity of the place is just staggering. He talks about how maybe he'll quit eating dairy and eggs because it seems like the right thing to do, and about seeing Lou Reed walking his tiny dog, and how he followed him until the dog took a shit just so he could watch Lou Reed pick up shit.

With my mouth full of food I tell him, "Yuh. Ah toelly gih thah," and he asks me what I'm eating. I swallow. "Uh, mac and cheese."

"From the box?"

"From the box."

"No, homie! From the fucking *box*? Come *on*! *Carnalito*, you can do better."

But at that moment, I'm so happy I don't know if I can.

Like you do with friends you don't see often, we begin retelling stories. We talk about people we knew, and we talk about shows we went to together. After a while we get around to talking about crimes. We talk about a night in our lives we've retold each other so many times and in so many different ways.

It's Little Italy a few months before Chente left San Diego. We meet up and we walk the streets with their expensive, candle-lit restaurants and fancy cafés, and we sip his flask of tequila. Chente says he's got a plan. "Homie, I got a plan for tonight. This place ... this whole shitty place and its plush Italian food owned by motherfuckers who aren't even Italian. We're going to Marco's because they're the worst culprit of all but their food ... you don't even know! If you can afford it, you're in heaven. The food is great, but honestly that place needs to *go*." We stop at the corner, and he zips up his canvas jacket (it's tight, narrow, he's lost a lot of weight because he's been living in his car down by Rose Creek and saving everything he has to move to New York). Chente looks for cops then pulls his flask out of his inside jacket pocket, tips it back, and hands it to me. "The eggplant parm?" he says. "Homie, you will *kill* yourself. You'll kill every fake motherfucker for a 60-block radius, especially whoever Marco is because, *compa*, the food? It's so good Marco deserves to *die*. I have it on good authority he doesn't even *exist*. There's no Marco. The place isn't even *owned* by Italians. We're gonna destroy it. We're going right now."

"Why do you care who owns it?"

"Why do I care? It's fake. I hate fake shit, and it's time to destroy."

"Destroying is the *last* thing I want to do right now," I tell him. "Destroying sounds *exhausting*."

"I don't care," he says. "Do it for rock 'n' roll. We're going right now, and I hope you're hungry."

At Marco's we're seated at a café table outside under a silver heater tower. We watch the late-night traffic go by. It's a beautiful night—a big white moon over the harbor so clear you can see the gray spots and rutted lines across its face. Just a breath of wind from the west and with it the smell of the sea.

Chente slumps low in his seat until he's practically lying down and stares up at the night's sky and I drink what's left of his tequila.

When the waitress brings the bread, we eat it with globs of butter.

When the bread is gone, we order more.

A few minutes later the waitress brings another basket of bread and asks what we want.

I start to say spaghetti with marinara because it's the cheapest thing on the menu, but Chente's like, "Nah, nope, trust me," and he turns to the waitress, who is wearing a spotless white blouse tucked into a black skirt, and says, "Two orders of eggplant parm."

"Sure, we can do that," she says, writing it on her notepad. "You want, like, um, some appetizers or anything?"

"More bread? If that's okay," I tell her.

"Sure. You can have as much as you want. Y'all want something to drink?"

Chente smiles, casual, relaxed, and puts his hands

behind his head, leaning back in his chair.

"What's your name?" he asks her.

"Monica."

"Know what, Monica? Bring us a bottle of your most expensive chianti, okay?"

"Y'all boys is crazy," she says laughing. She picks up the wine list from the table and looks at it. "We got a, like, a Castello Della .. I dunno how you say this, uh, Paneretta from 1998."

"You like it?" asks Chente.

"Nah, I never had it, but I hear it's good. They tell me it's good."

"Who's Marco? He Italian?"

"Nah," she laughs. "There ain't no Marco."

"Really? No Marco?"

She laughs again. "Yup. No Marco. It's just a name. He's like, um, like an imaginary boss."

"You got an imaginary boss, *mija*?"

She looks around, then says, quieter now, "*Between us*, I got an actual real boss, but I also got a Marco who's make-believe as shit."

"Who owns the place?"

"My ... um, my boss Brad," she says, twisting a length of hair in her fingers. "He's a piece of shit." She leans closer. "Muhfucker like fuckin' rubs up on me when he's in the kitchen."

"How *dare* he," says Chente. "Girl, Brad needs to get beat the fuck *down*."

"He's a piece of trash like for *real* for real."

"Brad's not Italian is he?"

The girl laughs and covers her mouth with her hand. "Who Brad?" she says quietly. "Nah, Brad's like ... he's like some classic San Diego, like—" here she puts on an exaggerated Californian accent "—like, yeah, brah, yeah, bro, hang ten, hang loose, like a surfer dude white guy. No offense," she says looking at me.

I tell her it's all good, because it is.

"Muhfucker's the least Italianest guy anywhere. He's got red hair. He's like some leprechaun Lucky Charms magically delicious pot a-gold muhfucker. Brad, like he's my *boss*, and everything, but Brad can suck my fuckin' dick."

"Alright, thanks," Chente says. "Thank you, Monica. You've been a big help. My friend and I here, we thank you."

"You boys crazy as shit. I like you. I like what you're doing here, you know that? I don't know what it is, but I approve."

When our dinner arrives, Chente asks the girl if he can tip in advance and she says, "Sure, yeah, I guess," and he gives her three twenties and says, "Here's the tip. Don't share it."

She thanks him, and heads back inside to get more bread.

The wine is light and airy and dry, and the eggplant parmesan is lovely—a dozen thin slices of eggplant breaded and baked to a deep golden brown covered in melted bright white mozzarella, a little red sauce streaked across the top but not too much, and parmesan grated over all of it with a bit of fresh basil. The eggplant is beautiful, robust, steaming in the night air. The slices fall apart in your mouth. They crumble into delicate, salty, buttery nothing. It's so good I want to cry for months, maybe years. Chente's right. It's so perfect I want to kill myself, but in a good way. First kill Brad of course as a tribute to Monica then I'll pull open my chest like Superman opening his shirt, and blinding light will shine out, and I will burst into a sunflash, and leave this shitty, sad life I have trudged through these 24 years. I will race through the cosmos as a new being of light and I will do so because of eggplant goddamn fucking *parm*.

As I'm marveling over the food, Chente stands, drops his green cloth napkin on the ground, picks up his plate from the table, and steps over the low guard rail.

"Wait, Chente," I say. "Where are you g—"

"Homie, let's *bounce*," he whispers. "Get your food. Come on!" and then he's around the corner with his plate in his hands and I'm behind him, holding my plate out in front of me.

Chente starts to run.

I follow.

A few days after my phone conversation with Chente, Frances Alicio ("Frankie" to our friends) sits across from me at the Old Spaghetti Factory in the Gaslamp. We're looking at our menus. "What are you getting?" she asks. I tell her just spaghetti and marinara, and she tells me she's thinking of fettuccini with browned butter and mizithra sauce, but that it doesn't matter because it's all about the spumoni ice cream they bring you at the end.

This is a date.

I think.

Sometimes it's a date when I don't know it's a date.

"No one really *dates* these days," I told my parents a few weeks ago over the phone. "People just kind of, like ... uh, get together. Friends you already know. It's better that way. It's not weird or awkward or anything."

All week I've wanted to die, but I'm still here. That feels like something. Still being here. Still being *of the world.*

Frankie sets her menu down on the table. The waiter is someone we know. I can't remember his name, and I don't think he remembers mine. He has blonde hair, and it's the same length as a lot of Frankie's friends, and sometimes they just blur together. At least five of them work at the Old Spaghetti Factory. They're nice guys, but they look like clones of each other. Which sounds nice—being clones with your friends, being so close to someone you become that person. The Old Spaghetti Clone Factory. It's wonderful. It's so sweet it starts to hurt my chest, and the thought of their lovely, tight-knit friendship wells up tears in my eyes, and I hold my menu in front of my face and pretend to look at it until I'm okay again.

Frankie and the waiter catch up for a while, talk about people they know, classes they're taking at Mesa, bands they've seen lately at the Ché or in the tunnels.

"Make sure to bring spumoni!" she says with a laugh as he walks away.

"You okay?" she asks me.

"Not at all," I say, and we both laugh.

"Yeah, fuck it, me either," she says.

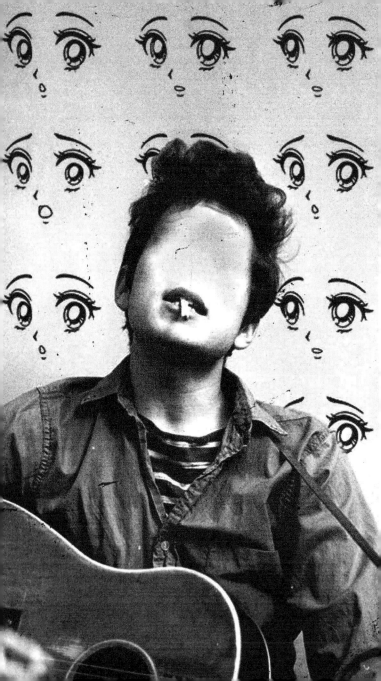

EPILOGUE

Hemingway wrote that Paris was a moveable feast but maybe any place or time or group of people can be if you love it or them well enough, if you remember the events clearly, and if you choose to carry their memory with you. Tonight I am thinking of those I'm so far from. I hold them with me as I maneuver through my days and I think often of how bad I thought it was at the time, how hard, how painful. Looking back, it wasn't. Maybe we never see a time clear enough to say What It Is when we're in the middle of it. Later, in hindsight, we can put it in a small, gold cardboard jeweler's box, and tie it up neatly with a bright green piece of yarn and say, "This was—" and fill in the blank. This was this, it was that, best of times, worst of times, glory days, dark ages, a perfect day where you made me forget myself or heavenly wine and roses ...

Last year the virus came into our lives, and took many of them. It stepped through our towns and cities like the fingers of an invisible hand. Taking us, staining us, pushing us to our ends. Now we stay in our homes. We talk to each other over computers and phones, and we say, "I love you so much and I'm *so* glad we got to talk" or "It was so nice hearing your voice" or "seeing your face" and we wait.

We wait. Some days it's pleasant. Alison and I cook wild, extravagant meals while records spin on the turntable. We take vitamins and drink a lot of water and we hope for the best. Twice we've been sick. Twice we've made it through. We cook recipes from Chente who is now a famous chef in New York City. We cook endless pasta and winy marinara with chewy, beautiful loaves of miche and pain de campagne from Wheatfields in Lawrence slathered in good, salty butter made from macadamia nuts. We cook casserole pans of English-style roast vegetables (and mushroom gravy with fresh herbs on the stove to pour over it). We cook pasta primavera with garlic butter sauce, and we do bread and tomato soup with our old sourdough. In the mornings—tacos or everything bagels with Miyoko's cream cheese and slices of avocado. Late at night, popcorn, almond butter from the jar for me, or leftover Christmas candy. After the food shortages began, we made sure to stock up. We have a lot of everything. Enough to last out this year and part of the next.

We are safe here on our farm in the country. Pantry stocked. A shotgun in the closet and many boxes of shells. We've got cases of canned black beans and corn, boxes of fancy udon soup left over from the first time we got the virus. Bouillon, pasta, rice, couscous, dried mushrooms, lentils, flour, and oil from the second. Most of our days are good days. We have it better than a lot of people.

Still, even on the happiest days, I think of the people I'm so far away from—everyone existing in their own small bubble, trying to keep healthy, hoping for the best, hoping their loved ones live, hoping that maybe next week or next month or next year this will all be over.

After tonight, everything will be different.

We dream of rebirth, victory, and renewal. We imagine we are just one quick step away from change and redemption. We love each other from afar and we try to stay in touch, but we're all still stuck in our own battles, so removed from whom we once were and where we walked the earth as children when we thought nothing would ever change. Now we hope for betterment and ascension. After tonight, everything will be different.

A few weeks ago, Frankie sent me a text with a YouTube link for the song "Bob Dylan's Dream" in which Dylan sings of days gone by and faces remembered but fading from view.

"I wish, I wish, I wish in vain
That we could sit simply in that room again
Ten thousand dollars at the drop of a hat
I'd give it all gladly if our lives could be like that"

So, this feast, this nightmare, this wonderful dream, this life we have lived we clutch like a great burlap sack of dry bones thrown over our shoulder, carried on our back. We heft it from place to place, and sometimes we hate it for its burden, but sometimes we open it up and pick through the old, long bones, and maybe we find something we remember. On some nights, nights when it is very quiet, and we feel as if no one is watching, we breathe life back into what we once had and sometimes those bones stand right up, walk around, and dance for just a bit.

ACKNOWLEDGEMENTS

****

This book was inspired by Stanley Tucci and Joseph Tropiano's *Big Night*, M.F.K. Fisher's *The Gastronomical Me* and *How to Cook a Wolf*, Anthony Bourdain's books *Kitchen Confidential* and *A Cook's Tour*, Liam and Jack Christian, Angelo Pappas, Rich Baiocco, Giancarlo DiTrapano, Dutch Renaissance and Flemish painting, Lou Reed's *Transformer*, Gustav Adolf Ekdahl, Henry Miller, *Moonstruck*, Raymond Cappomaggi, Charles Dickens, Sandra Cisneros, and Rudy Ramos' Vegicano recipes. Also important: Beethoven's *Piano Concerto No. 1 in C Major, Op. 15* and the *Sonata No. 27 in E Minor, Op. 90*, which I listened to while writing the book and which you are meant to listen to as you read it (if you truly want to do it right). Eternal thanks goes out to the editorial, design, photography, research, fact-checking, publishing team of Jessie Duke, Bran Black Moon, Reira Moon, Elizabeth Thompson, Becky DiGiglio, and Justin Pearson. Endless respect to Bart Schaneman, Nathaniel Kennon Perkins, Nicole Morning, Erik Henriksen, Jon Nix, Ryan Bradford, Jessie Lynn McMains, Lora Mathis, Julia Dixon Evans, Rich Baiocco, Nick Bernal, Mallory Smart, Eileen Ramos, Giacomo Pope, Joshua Bohnsack, Dmitry Samarov, Paul DeGeorge, and Michael J. Seidlinger for their help, encouragement, and good suggestions. *After Tonight, Everything Will Be Different* was written in isolation during the second year of the COVID-19 virus and finished in suite #201 of the Leavenworth Local hotel. Suite #201 is the former chapel of the Immaculata High School and is known as "the Wall of Light." Sincere thanks to the staff of the Leavenworth Local for their hospitality, patience, and discretion.

This book is for Elizabeth.

ABOUT THE AUTHOR

****

Born and raised in San Diego, California, Adam Gnade now lives on the Ruby Teeth Homestead in the rural Midwest. His books and audio recordings of writing share characters and plotlines in an attempt to build a vast universe documenting how it was to live in the time that he was alive. The ongoing collected series is titled *We Live Nowhere and Know No One,* and continues in a variety of novels, novellas, and writing released on vinyl and cassette.

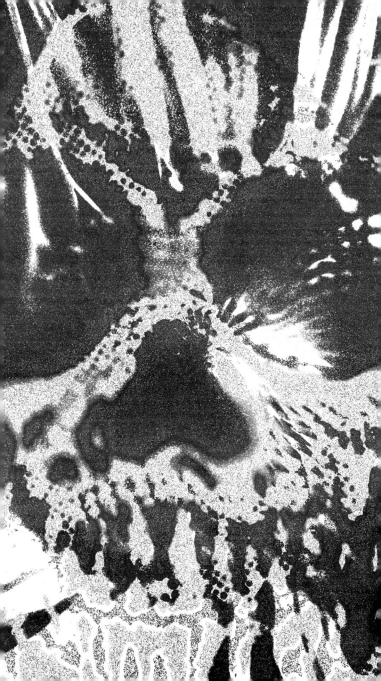

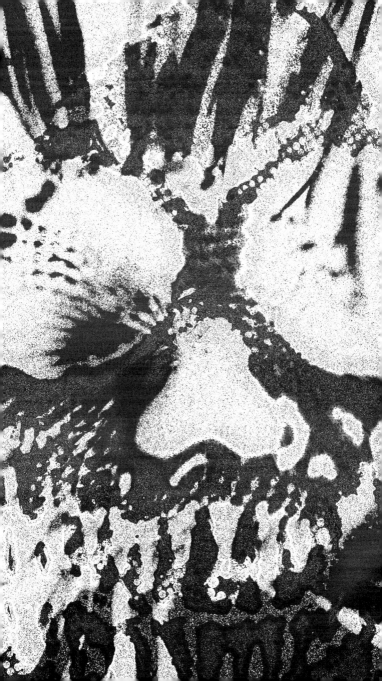